Lila suddenly drew ——— ou think I'm crazy!" she cried, nodding violently. "That's what Theodore told Flora. He told her that she was crazy—"

"Stop it!" Damon shouted. "Stop it! Stop it!"

"He hurt her! He threw things at her and threatened her with a knife!" Lila shouted.

"Is that what you *want*, then?" Damon cried, grabbing her and shaking her. Sweat poured off his face, and he could feel the muscles in his arms violently thrusting her back and forth. He felt strangely disconnected from his body. His rational mind was incapable of stopping the rage that had taken over.

Lila began screaming, but her screams only urged him on.

"Is that why you're telling me all of these crazy stories?" Damon shouted. He grabbed a hunk of her hair and yanked her head back so that he could look directly into her terrified brown eyes. "Do you really think that I am Theodore and that you are Flora? Do you want me to hurt you the way you imagine *he* hurt her?"

Lila let out a long wail and beat his chest with her fists. "You're just trying to make me think I'm going crazy!"

"Should I beat you up? Would that prove you're right?" Damon shrieked. *"What do you want from me, Flora?"*

Bantam Books in the Sweet Valley University series.
Ask your bookseller for the books you have missed.

And don't miss these Sweet Valley University Thriller Editions:

Visit the Official Sweet Valley Web Site on the Internet at:

http://www.sweetvalley.com

SWEET VALLEY UNIVERSITY®

THRILLER EDITION

Love and Murder

Written by
Laurie John

Created by
FRANCINE PASCAL

BANTAM BOOKS
NEW YORK · TORONTO · LONDON · SYDNEY · AUCKLAND

To Margaret Abigail Chardiet

RL 8, age 14 and up

LOVE AND MURDER
A Bantam Book / May 1998

Sweet Valley High® and Sweet Valley University®
are registered trademarks of Francine Pascal.
Conceived by Francine Pascal.
Produced by Daniel Weiss Associates, Inc.
33 West 17th Street
New York, NY 10011.

ISBN: 0-553-49225-X

Published simultaneously in the United States and Canada

Bantam Books are published by Bantam Books, a division of Bantam
Doubleday Dell Publishing Group, Inc. Its trademark, consisting of the
words "Bantam Books" and the portrayal of a rooster, is Registered in
U.S. Patent and Trademark Office and in other countries. Marca
Registrada. Bantam Books, 1540 Broadway, New York, New York 10036.

PRINTED IN THE UNITED STATES OF AMERICA

OPM   0 9 8 7 6 5 4 3 2 1

Chapter One

"The thick, encrusted surfaces and deliberately clumsy draftsmanship of the Brücke group show that they rejected all artistic refinement in favor of direct, primitive expression. . . ."

Lila Fowler felt her eyes glaze over as Professor Heckman clicked the button on his slide projector. She slid one slender elbow out on her chair's writing arm and cupped her chin in her hand.

"Note the lack of detailed expression in Kirchner's faces—like grotesque masks in a . . ."

Grotesque *is definitely the word I'd use,* Lila thought miserably. She checked her delicate Tiffany watch. *Nine-fifteen A.M. and I'm stuck in my Twentieth-Century Art lecture alone. Where's Jessica?*

Lila sighed and stared down at the glossy Midnight Red nail polish she'd applied last night. *Thank goodness I didn't let one of those Brücke painters do my nails. They would have been a mess.*

As Professor Heckman droned on, Lila looked up momentarily from her nails. Heckman was short and balding, with baggy pockets in his jacket that held his greasy notepads and pencils. Pacing back and forth in front of the screen, he looked like a nervous bird on a branch wondering where his next worm was going to come from.

Lila shook the image away and crossed her legs. Just a few short months ago she'd been perfectly happy, lying on the beach along the Italian Riviera with the new husband she adored, the Count Tisiano di Mondicci. Together they'd roamed through the finest museums and galleries in Europe, viewing and buying paintings a thousand times better than the ones Professor Heckman was raving about.

Now he was dead and she was back in Sweet Valley, California, unhappily making like a proper Sweet Valley University undergrad in a dusty lecture hall very, *very* early in the morning. She looked over her shoulder toward the door, then sank back into her seat. Not even her best friend, Jessica Wakefield, was there to console her.

Another slide appeared, showing a messy, unattractive oil that appeared to have been painted by a group of kindergartners. Lila looked away again and dug into her purse for a nail file, determined to make some good use of the time. The teeniest chip had begun to appear on the corner of her right index fingernail.

She was still rummaging through the bottom of her purse when the lights suddenly flared on.

"We'll be moving on to a more detailed discussion of the Brücke movement at this point," Professor Heckman croaked into his microphone. "And taking over for me will be my new teaching assistant, Mr. Damon Price, who is an authority on this period."

Oooh, Lila thought distractedly, accidentally pulling a pencil from her purse instead of a nail file. She threw it back in irritation. *Another moldy old art authority. I can't wait to hear what he says.*

"Ms. Fowler? Lila? Are you with us this morning?" she heard Professor Heckman call out.

Lila froze, looked up, and felt a hundred pairs of eyes burning into her. But then, as her eyes began to focus on the lectern at the front of the room, she felt a zap go through her body like a raw bolt of electricity.

Standing next to her professor was a tall, striking man in his early twenties. He had dark, rumpled hair and tortoiseshell-rimmed glasses that only partly disguised the classically handsome features of his face. He wore a denim shirt, a corduroy jacket, and a pair of jeans. Lila's lips parted slightly. When the new TA leaned up against the lectern to look at the class, he slipped off the glasses, revealing clear, quizzical eyes that seemed to immediately connect with hers.

3

Lila practically stopped breathing as her senses seemed to focus acutely on the face before her. She knew she had never seen him before, but there was something familiar in the high, serious brow and the slow smile that began to creep out of the corner of his mouth.

Lila cleared her throat. "Yes, Professor Heckman. I'm here."

"Pleased to hear that," her professor continued. "Mr. Price has just returned from an extensive research trip through Europe, where he has been studying the expressionists, and has also completed some fascinating research on the surrealist movement and its relationship to the . . ."

Lila's eyes were still fixed on the new TA's face. Her hand made a sudden, nervous move to brush back her hair, but as she did so she heard a crash and looked down in horror. She had forgotten that her open purse had been poised on the writing arm of her chair. Now it lay on the floor, and its contents were spilling everywhere. Lipsticks rolled under the rows of seats in front of her. A gold-plated compact clattered and broke noisily. A bulging coin purse burst open, sending coins rolling in every direction.

She could feel her face redden with intense embarrassment.

The new TA set his elbows down on the lectern, and let his eyes rest curiously on her.

A few students began giggling softly behind

Lila, and she stirred uncomfortably in her seat. "Please excuse me, Mr. . . . um . . ."

"Price," the TA said instantly, his deep green eyes still locked on hers. "Damon Price. And you'd better put that in your notes if you're taking any. Because you *will* be quizzed on it later."

The class tittered.

Lila shuddered, looking away. The whole horrible moment was turning into one of the worst humiliations of her life. But when she looked up again, she noticed that he was still staring at her and had not begun his lecture.

She returned his gaze boldly and saw that on the surface, his expression was stern. But as she looked deeper into his eyes she saw a glint that made her wonder. Was that a look of pleased amusement that just flashed over his face?

Or was it just her imagination?

Jessica Wakefield angled her lovely face up into the sun, swept her blond hair back over her shoulders, and sighed. Sunny mornings like this one were perfect for skipping class, especially classes taught by moldy old professors like Dr. Heckman.

Poor Lila, Jessica thought, curling her tanned legs under her as she leaned back on one arm and stared up at the window of her art history lecture hall. *Whatever made her hide herself away in class on a day like this?*

She eyed a group of bare-chested guys who were heading out onto the lawn for a game of Frisbee. One blond-haired guy with an especially white set of teeth gave her a brilliant smile as he flung the disk behind his back.

Jessica tossed him a smile before stretching out her legs and rolling onto her stomach. The university quad was a great place to sunbathe. She liked its long, carefully manicured stretch of grass and trees. It was dotted with benches and bordered on three sides by stucco buildings with quaint, red-tiled roofs.

She poked her nose back into the nice trashy novel she'd brought with her. On its cover a voluptuous woman in a low-cut satin dress was draped across the arms of a ruggedly handsome man wearing a torn, ruffled shirt.

"Jessica! *Jessica!*"

Jessica propped herself up on her elbow and glanced in the direction of the familiar voice. Lila Fowler was hurrying down the middle of the university quad as if she were being pursued by the entire Neiman Marcus sales staff. Jessica narrowed her eyes. What was wrong with her?

Today, Jessica noted, Lila was wearing an immaculately cut, sleeveless linen pantsuit, one of the many outfits Lila had acquired in European boutiques during her whirlwind courtship and marriage to the Count di Mondicci. But her thick chestnut hair was whipping wildly around her face, and her porcelain complexion was pink with excitement.

"Jes-si-ca . . ." Lila panted, dropping down on the grass next to her. She stopped to catch her breath. "You shouldn't have skipped Twentieth-Century Art."

Jessica eyed her. "Why?" she said dryly. "Did Professor Heckman turn into a prince after you kissed him?"

Lila drew up her slender knees and hugged them, her face uncharacteristically flushed and her eyes burning. "Something along those lines."

"What?" Jessica sat up, snapping shut her romance novel. Lila Fowler had actually *kissed* Professor Heckman? Exactly *what* could she have possibly kissed? His cheek? His hand? His horrid bald spot? She shuddered at the thought. She never imagined Lila would go *that* far to get a good grade.

Lila's brown eyes glazed over. "Professor Heckman brought in a new TA for the class, and he's the most incredibly gorgeous guy I've ever seen in my life."

Jessica felt her mouth drop open.

"He's very tall and tanned," Lila went on breathlessly. "And he has these very green eyes and . . . once we started looking at each other, Jessica, it was like we couldn't tear our eyes away."

"I don't believe it," Jessica said. "This was in *Professor Heckman's* class? World headquarters for the most boring learning approaches to art history?"

7

"Yes!" Lila gushed. "Oh, it was *incredible.*"

Sure, it's incredible, Jessica thought miserably. *Just like it was incredible when you met and actually married the Count di Mondicci. Why do you have all the luck?*

"We *connected,* Jessica," Lila said solemnly, resting her delicate chin on her knees.

"What do you mean, you *connected?*" Jessica demanded.

"It means"—Lila sighed—"that I've only seen him once and that I've never even had a conversation with him, but *something* has happened."

Jessica looked closely at Lila's face. She could actually see stars shimmering in her friend's eyes.

"It's something important," Lila breathed. "I've heard about this kind of thing happening between two people, but I never thought it would happen to me."

Jessica looked at her skeptically. "Excuse me, Lila. But don't you already have a boyfriend?"

"I know," Lila said dreamily.

"Some guy named Bruce Patman who's conveniently studying in *Japan* right now?" Jessica went on. "You've been slavishly devoted to him for months now, remember?"

Lila flushed. "This doesn't have anything to do with Bruce."

"Yes, it does," Jessica reminded her. "And I don't believe you could actually be in love after seeing this guy for five minutes."

Lila's eyes remained glazed over. "When you connect with a guy like this, you have to see it through even if you *do* happen to be going out with someone else."

"I'll remember to tell Bruce that when he comes back," Jessica drawled.

Lila looked unfazed. "Come to the next class, Jessica. You'll see what I mean."

"I wouldn't miss it for the world."

Smiling dizzily, Lila jumped to her feet. "Gotta go."

"Don't trip all over yourself."

Lila seemed oblivious. "Catch you for dinner at the student union at six, OK?"

"Yeah," Jessica murmured thoughtfully as she watched Lila wander away down the quad. "And thanks for ruining my morning, Lila."

Jessica pressed her lips together. From what she could tell, Lila really *had* fallen instantly for this guy, which was pretty incredible considering Lila's naturally cool and wary personality. Jessica shook her head. *I'd be cool and wary too if I were drop-dead gorgeous and had millions in my bank account*, she mused. *So what's up with her now?*

She jammed her paperback into her backpack and stood up, flipping back one thick strand of blond hair. "Well, don't expect my bad mood to last, Lila," she murmured schemingly. "I'll be there next Wednesday, and I will *definitely* be looking my best. Once our new TA takes one look at me, he'll know which work of art he appreciates more."

"Directory assistance for Sweet Valley," the operator stated sourly.

"Price," Lila said, tapping her cordless phone with an impatient, glossy fingernail. "First name, Damon."

"One moment, please."

Lila's pencil was poised over the *P* section of her thick address book and her heart was pumping wildly. She looked out her apartment window at the falling light through the trees. It had been only nine hours since she'd last seen Professor Heckman's mysterious new teaching assistant, but she wasn't about to wait until next week to see him again.

Lila Fowler was not used to being kept waiting, after all.

"I'm sorry," the operator finally said. "I have no listing in the Sweet Valley region for anyone by that name."

Lila gritted her teeth. "Last name, Price. First name, Damon."

"I've tried *P-r-i-c-e* and *P-r-y-c-e,* and neither name is listed under the first name Damon or initial *D* or any first name beginning with the letter *D.*"

"Well, I commend you for being so irritatingly thorough," Lila snapped before clicking the phone off hard with her thumb and falling backward on her fluffy bed.

Lila tried to think. Damon Price. Teaching assistant. Maybe they'd given him a private office with his own phone. With any luck he'd have one already.

Without hesitating, she clicked on the phone again and dialed the university operator.

"SVU switchboard."

"I need the number for a teaching assistant named Damon Price," Lila asked politely.

"Just a minute, please."

Lila stared up at the ceiling. *I'm so crazy. I'm so crazy,* she thought anxiously.

"Oh. OK," the operator began. "Mr. Price's number is 555–9045."

Lila quickly jotted down the number. "Thank you," she said triumphantly, feeling a stab of excitement in the pit of her stomach. She steadied herself, then punched the number.

"Hello. You've reached the voice mailbox of Damon Price," Damon's deep voice announced. *"Please leave a message after the tone, and I'll return your call as soon as I can."*

Lila took a deep breath and closed her eyes. "Hello, Mr. Price. This is Lila Fowler from Professor Heckman's Twentieth-Century Art class. I wanted to personally apologize for disturbing your introduction this morning. But there was one other thing too. . . ." Lila bit her lower lip and concentrated. "During my travels in Europe I took a special interest in the Brücke group myself," she lied. "In fact, I'm doing further research on . . . uh, Claude Monet right now and wondered if we could meet one-on-one to discuss it. My number is 555–9934."

By this time Lila could barely breathe; just thinking about Damon Price's face and the fact that he would be listening to her message within a matter of hours—if not minutes—made her panic.

"Well," Lila said quickly. "I look forward to hearing from you soon, then. Good-bye, Damon, for now."

Lila pressed the Off button on her cordless phone. The room was cool, but her back was damp with sweat. Her racing heart had begun to slow, but she could barely move a muscle, as if she'd just run a marathon.

Her eyes traveled to the small table beside her bed, where she'd arranged silver-framed photos of the people she loved most in life: Jessica, Isabella Ricci, her parents, and her boyfriend, Bruce. The largest one was of her beloved late husband, Tisiano—a shot she'd taken on their honeymoon on their private yacht in Greece. She stared at his tanned face and inexpressibly happy smile against a backdrop of sapphire blue sky. She'd loved Tisiano so much, and yet she had always known that a distance existed between them—even in their passion.

What Lila had detected in Damon's eyes was something completely different from what she'd known with Tisiano and Bruce. She'd known it from the moment their eyes had connected. There was a current running between them. A bond she couldn't explain.

I've never spoken to him, Lila thought. *And yet I feel as if I've known him for a very long time.*

"What'll it be?" the SVU Pub bartender asked, wiping down the bar with a white cloth.

Damon Price slid his briefcase up onto the bar and rubbed his jaw. "Give me any kind of good, dark beer. Surprise me."

The bartender nodded.

Damon clicked open his briefcase and dragged out several notebooks. After assisting with Professor Heckman's seminar that morning, he'd taught two art appreciation classes. Then he had three student conferences and a faculty meeting. Tonight he had to prepare his notes for next week's Twentieth-Century lecture, and the SVU Pub was a good, laid-back place to do it.

After the bartender poured the beer and walked away, Damon took a sip, set down the mug, then stretched his neck. Sure, the hours were long, but there definitely were worse things in life than landing an assistant teaching job at a big university like this one.

He shook his head and pulled out the first part of his doctoral dissertation he'd written on the surrealists when he was in Europe. Professor Heckman had actually read it and praised him. Now he planned to use it for part of his lecture next week.

OK, here's the point where I trace Man Ray's shift from painting to photography, he noted. *Now if I could just find that reference I made to . . .*

He felt his thoughts drifting away, though he wasn't sure where they were headed. He'd been feeling weird all day. He felt suddenly as if he were home, even though he was a good three thousand miles away from it. For some reason he had a sense of belonging in Sweet Valley, as if he were connected to someone near.

He looked around. Through the dim light he could see dozens of students, crowded around the bar and the pub's small tables, talking intently and laughing. Soft jazz played in the background, and there were books everywhere. He didn't recognize a soul in here, and yet . . .

Damon searched for a pencil in his briefcase and drew out a sheet of fresh paper, ready to begin outlining his next lecture. But his thoughts just wouldn't focus. He doodled aimlessly, searching his mind for something to hook onto—a clue to his strange feelings.

"Get you something else?" the bartender asked. "We've got a special on the combo pizza."

"No, thanks," Damon said absently, pushing a lock of unruly hair out of his eyes.

14

"What are you drawing?" the waiter asked, craning his neck around.

Damon frowned, then looked down at the paper in front of him. A strange longing shot through him. His doodling had actually produced a sketch, the rough outline of a woman's face. For a few moments he just stared at it. There were the eyes, stern yet catlike. The full lips. The warm curve of a cheek. The thick hair that tumbled forward over her shoulders.

"I'm drawing a portrait," Damon replied slowly as his amazement grew. "It's of a woman I just saw today."

The waiter chuckled. "Oh, really? She didn't tell you her name, huh?"

Damon stared deeper into the picture, drawn to it as if he were remembering the strand of a faraway dream.

"Not exactly," Damon replied softly. "But I do know her name is Lila."

Chapter Two

"Why hasn't he called?" Lila murmured to herself, taking one last sip of cappuccino.

She looked out the window at the cloudless blue sky. Her off-campus apartment was actually a small, early-California-style cottage, one of several arranged around a central, landscaped courtyard, each with its own private porch. It was a far cry from the cramped dorm rooms most of her friends lived in on the SVU campus, Lila knew. But then, she could easily afford it.

Plus Lila wasn't used to sharing, like her friends Jessica and Isabella were. She was the only child of wealthy parents. And after Tisiano died, she, of course, had inherited millions of her own. But Lila wasn't thinking about money as she padded down the hallway to pick out an outfit.

She was thinking about Damon Price.

I've given him plenty of time to call back, she

thought. *So why am I still lurking next to the phone?*

All night she'd tossed and turned, wondering what they would say to each other when he returned her call. That is, if he ever *did* return her call. She'd actually stayed home all morning waiting for the phone to ring, but now it was almost lunch, and she was due at the Theta Alpha Theta sorority house for a special committee meeting.

Lila laid out an Irish linen pantsuit, studied it carefully, then pulled a flowing, sleeveless dress from her closet instead. Matching calfskin shoes followed, and from her jewelry box she chose a priceless eighteenth-century silver pendant Tisiano had bought for her in Venice. Finally she applied a coat of fresh lipstick before grabbing her leather bag and heading out the door.

"The mail," she murmured, turning around and stepping back up to her little brick porch. She took out her mailbox key and opened it, pulling out several bills, a stack of clothing and jewelry catalogs, and an airmail letter with Bruce Patman's return address on it.

Interesting timing, Bruce, Lila thought, slamming the box shut and heading out toward Theta house. She slipped everything but Bruce's letter in her purse, then carefully tore the corner of the envelope with her teeth.

She turned onto the sidewalk, walking slowly as she pulled a photograph from the envelope. It was a picture of Bruce, sitting on a rock in what

17

looked like a Japanese garden, flanked by two Japanese guys. Lila smiled. In the photo Bruce's head was thrown back in laughter, and his dark hair was blowing across his tanned forehead.

Lila stared intently at the photo. Bruce had left nearly a month ago for a special semester-abroad program for econ majors at the University of Kyoto. *He looks happy,* she thought with a pang. *Really happy.*

She slipped the note out of the envelope.

Dear Lila,

You're always telling me to smile, so you can see why I'm sending you this particular shot. Check out my buds, a couple of guys from the dorm who started hanging out with me to improve their English. Now they've got me speaking a few words of their own language. Thanks, Kato and Aki. Japan is great—even better than I thought it would be. But one essential thing is missing: you. I miss you, Lila. All the time I'm sitting through another jam-packed lecture or trying to eat octopus, I'm thinking of you. The nights are hardest, Li. Write me soon, and know that I am counting the days until I see you again.

Love, Bruce

Lila felt hot tears behind her eyes, but she blinked them back and crossed University Avenue, still holding the letter and photo in her hand.

That's the sweetest letter anyone's ever sent me in my life, Lila thought guiltily. So sweet, in fact, that Lila was having a hard time believing it was from Bruce. She glanced at it again, as if she wanted to make sure. A car whizzed by, and she carefully tucked the letter and photo back into the envelope and slipped the whole thing into her notebook.

A tree-lined side street to her right was where most of the SVU Greek houses were. Guilty thoughts began to creep into her head as she walked slowly past big Sigma house—Bruce's fraternity. Sure, Bruce was a spoiled-rotten rich kid with a reputation for arrogance, irresponsibility, and intense good looks. But what of it? So was she. Maybe they really *were* meant for each other.

But then a picture of Damon Price's face began to form in her mind. There was something so right in his eyes. So strangely familiar . . .

Get a clue, Lila, she scolded herself. *You've never even talked to Damon Price. Who knows if you even have a sliver of a chance with him?*

When Lila finally reached the front steps of Theta house, she'd managed to shove her thoughts of Damon into the back of her head. Bruce Patman, after all, was probably her perfect match. He understood her. He obviously loved her. And she was probably stuck with him—for better or for worse.

Wasn't she?

*   *   *

"How did the Art 201 seminar go today?" Professor Heckman asked Damon as the two walked up a flight of stairs in ancient Denton Hall.

"Great," Damon enthused, pushing his glasses up on his nose and breathing in the pleasant, chalky smell of the academic building. It was late afternoon, and he had just finished teaching two back-to-back introductory art classes. "It's a well-prepared group. And they seem to love the modern art period as much as I do."

Professor Heckman winked. "That why I wanted you to take over, Damon. Leave me to the classical periods, thank you. That's where this old bird is most comfortable."

Damon gave the old man a warm smile as they walked down the third-floor row of cramped faculty offices. "I appreciate the opportunity you're giving me to teach here, Professor Heckman. I don't know if I've ever properly thanked you."

Professor Heckman waved away the compliment. "It may turn out that I need you more than you need me, young man."

Damon stopped before the frosted glass pane of his office door. "I doubt that, sir. I spent a lot of time doing my research in Europe, but it wasn't half as challenging as teaching is."

"Just try to keep focused, and you'll be fine," Professor Heckman said, patting him on the back. "Keep your eyes off those pretty girls too." He

20

winked again. "It can do crazy things to the mind, especially when you're as young as you are."

Damon winced inwardly as he waved good-bye and unlocked the door to his own, closet-size, book-lined office. He dumped his briefcase on the nearest chair and took off his jacket, pausing as his eyes rested on the print he'd just hung on the far wall.

It was a copy of a surrealist work painted over half a century earlier by a now obscure artist whose merit Damon was trying to bring attention to. One of the reasons he'd hung it up was because his office had no window.

The picture, however, was of a view through a window frame. White clouds hung in a deep blue sky. That was all.

Damon stared at it. The picture always had a way of calming him and stimulating him at the same time. He loved the cool blue of the sky behind the layers of cloud and the mysterious way the clouds appeared to shift if you looked at the painting long enough, revealing the face of a beautiful woman.

Only this time the play of cloud on sky was even stranger than it had ever been. In fact, Damon began to shudder as the outline of the face began to sharpen. He knew that face. It had a name attached to it now.

Lila.

No wonder I can't get her out of my mind, he realized. *She's been there all along.*

Damon sank down into the chair behind his

desk in a daze, searching for pencil and paper among the unpacked book boxes, ungraded papers, and empty coffee cups. He absently punched his office phone to receive the messages from his voice mailbox, which was already stuffed with excuses for late papers, invitations to faculty luncheons, and crazy messages from his painter friends in New York.

Then, just as his eyes lifted back to the painting, he heard a familiar, tentative voice on the machine.

"Hello, Mr. Price. This is Lila Fowler from Professor Heckman's Twentieth-Century Art class. I wanted to personally apologize for disturbing your introduction this morning. . . ."

Damon felt his chest begin to pound.

". . . wondered if we could meet one-on-one to discuss it. My number is 555–9934."

Damon quickly scribbled the phone number, turned off his voice mail, and looked up at the woman's face in the clouds. The face he wondered about and longed for. The face he could see with his eyes closed. The girl he was about to finally meet.

He picked up the phone's receiver and stared at it. He swallowed hard. The old bookshelves that surrounded him seemed to lean forward and close in on him. He searched his mind for something he could say to her, but the voices in his head confused him.

Damon raked back his hair with one hand. Voices.

Were they warning him—or were they urging him on?

A moment later Damon dropped the receiver back down and looked at his watch. He couldn't do it right now. He would wait a few hours, calm down, and try again.

Jessica hurried up the front steps of the Theta Alpha Theta house. Although it was supposed to be her usual kick-back lunch hour, she was now due at a meeting of a stupid Theta charity committee Lila had railroaded her into joining. She yanked open the front door and blew her bangs up irritably, forcing herself to remember how desperately she'd wanted to be selected for the exclusive sorority at the beginning of the year.

My entire lunch hour wasted, Jessica thought, tromping into the impressive front entry of the house, *all because of Lila*.

"Hi, Jessica," Isabella Ricci said with a languid smile. She was stretched out on the sofa in the Theta parlor, her silky black hair spilling luxuriously over her white cashmere sweater. "Ready to talk about charity fund-raiser development?"

"Can't wait," Jessica moped, flopping into an overstuffed chair. She stared up at the ceiling. "Isn't Lila here yet?"

"Of course not," Isabella said, flipping a page of her fashion magazine.

Hmmm, where could she be? Jessica wondered

bitterly. *Maybe she got picked up by the sap patrol on the way to the meeting. Charged with first-degree romantic faux pas: falling deeply and dopily in love with someone you know absolutely zilch about.*

"But Denise and Alex are here," Isabella said. "They're in the kitchen, trying to find something for us to eat."

Jessica rolled her eyes and stirred impatiently in her seat. The Thetas' president, Magda Helperin, and her vice dictator, Alison Quinn, had practically forced Lila, Isabella, Denise Waters, and Alexandra Rollins to form this special committee. Then Lila had strong-armed Jessica into joining too.

Jessica glowered into space. The meeting was sure to be dull: plans for the coming year's charity projects. *That's all I need,* Jessica thought bitterly. Midterms were next week, her love life was totally stalled while her best friend's was heating up, and here she was, stuck with the Thetas, talking about do-gooder projects.

And if *that* weren't enough, Lila hadn't even showed yet.

Denise and Alex finally entered the room, carrying a plastic tray of crackers and some dry-looking cheese.

"Hi, Jessica," Denise said, sitting down cross-legged on the sofa next to Isabella and dusting cracker crumbs off her ripped jeans. Her dark hair was pulled back off her face, revealing her direct blue eyes. "Have you seen Lila yet?"

"Nope," Jessica said glumly, crossing her arms.

"Well, let's get to work," Denise said. "The main item on our committee's agenda is establishing our charity works for the coming year."

Isabella and Alex nodded and began to look serious.

"Does anyone want to make a proposal?" Denise asked.

Jessica rolled her eyes again.

Alex sat up. "The Sweet Valley Family Shelter is expanding next year to include a soup kitchen. I'd like to propose that we help fund and staff the project."

Ugh, Jessica thought. *Work in a soup kitchen? Who's she trying to kid?*

Jessica watched with a stony face as Denise took suggestions ranging from helping senior citizens to volunteering at the local animal shelter.

There were footsteps in the hallway, and Jessica could hear Theta president Magda Helperin calling out brightly, "Lila! How *are* you? Are you here for your committee meeting?"

Jessica gritted her teeth. She hated the way the Thetas sucked up to Lila just because she had been an authentic Italian countess and had grown up with unbelievable wealth and connections. Most of the sisters in the room had clawed their way into Theta house. But Lila had actually been *recruited*.

If any other Theta had strolled into a meeting ten minutes late, Magda would have dressed her

25

down in front of the group and forced her into extra house chores, such as cleaning silver or weeding the flower beds.

Jessica watched Denise, Alex, and Isabella's faces brighten as Lila strolled into the parlor.

"Oh, Lila," Denise said. "I'm glad you could make it."

"Have I missed much?" Lila chirped.

"Not really. We're just talking about possible charity efforts and fund-raising ideas for next year," Isabella offered.

Jessica glared at Lila. She knew her too well. Lila had that spacey kitten look on her face. The one she always got when she was in love. Now she appeared to be half floating on the folding chair Magda had just brought in for her, her eyes glazed over as if she'd just put a very large and delicious chocolate into her mouth and was waiting for it to melt.

I can't stand it, Jessica thought darkly. *Lila already has a rich, handsome boyfriend. Now she's on the brink of finding another one! It's so disgusting!*

"Lila?" Denise asked.

The group started to giggle softly.

"Well," Lila said dreamily. "In Italy, Tisiano's family had a wonderful tradition. Each year they would open the house in Florence and hold a huge masked ball. It was a charity event to raise money for the restoration of old paintings."

There was a murmur of approval.

"Of course everyone loves a masked ball," Lila went on. "The di Mondicci family knew this and took advantage. The costumes were extravagant, but so were the ticket prices. They raised millions of lira for art each year."

Jessica crossed her legs. "But Lila," she said sweetly. "Not many students at SVU can afford a high-priced costume ball. Who would come besides you?"

Jessica heard the soft beginnings of giggles, but they were quickly extinguished by Lila's matter-of-fact reply. "The *alumni*, of course. I'm talking about alumni weekend. We've got the only decent ballroom on Greek Row. We could promote this as the main event of the season and raise thousands without any trouble."

"Sounds like a blast," Isabella murmured.

"My mother would love to show off with a big donation and a fabulous dress," Denise whispered.

"I already know what I'm going to wear." Alex giggled softly.

Jessica sat back in her chair, frustrated. She hated Lila for making her feel this—well, this *second-class*. Why was it that Lila always got the fascinating men, all the money in the world for clothes, and now the most popular idea in the room? It made Jessica want to bring Lila back down to earth—and hard.

Jessica watched in silence as the meeting proceeded through a list of possible charity recipients, fund-raiser dates, and budget matters. Meanwhile

Jessica kept looking back at Lila, whose expression of mild interest never seemed to change. Only her brown eyes seemed to fluctuate, from slow burn to fiery bright. Was Jessica the only one who knew how far away her thoughts were?

"This meeting is adjourned," Denise finally announced, standing up. "We will be discussing Lila's masked ball concept further at next Thursday's house meeting."

Jessica stood up and turned around just in time to see Lila float out of the room without saying a word to anyone. Her notebook, clasped loosely under her elbow, opened slightly as she turned the corner, releasing an envelope fringed along the edges with red and blue stripes. Jessica hurried forward as Lila's envelope fell to the ground, then stooped to pick it up.

For a moment Jessica just stood there, staring at the exotic Japanese stamp and the return address in the upper-left-hand corner: Bruce Patman, Akiama Hall, Room 401, University of Kyoto, Kyoto-Fu, 610–03, Japan.

Then, after quietly looking around to see if anyone had noticed, she slipped the envelope into her pocket.

"Sorry, Lila," Jessica murmured, "but I just have to keep this. After all, you never know. It might come in handy for me one day."

Damon was starting to feel foolish. It was five o'clock in the afternoon, and it was time for him to head home. Yet he was staying late in his office, reading through student papers, all on the off chance that Lila might call him back.

"This is crazy," he muttered to himself, shoving a paper away and raking his hair back with his fingers. "I don't even know who she is."

He stood up and paced the room, his hands stuffed deep into his trouser pockets.

You're twenty-three years old, he told himself. *You should know better by now.*

Damon shook his head, remembering the entanglements that had distracted him during his studies abroad the year before. He'd broken up with a beautiful painter he'd met in London just before landing his job at Sweet Valley University, vowing to devote himself solely to his teaching and research for at least two years. Now he found himself wanting to throw that promise to the wind—all because of this strange feeling he had about a woman he didn't even know.

Before Damon's thoughts could go any further, the phone rang, and he rushed to his desk to pick it up.

"Yes?" he said, managing his most sober voice.

"Hello. Is this Mr. Price?"

Damon felt a smile forming on his face, and the smile grew wider. *Lila.* A surge of adrenaline shot through his body. "Yes, it is," he replied.

"This is Lila Fowler. Um, I called earlier and left a message? Then you called me back today, but I wasn't home."

Damon's pulse raced. "Oh yes. I'm glad we finally connected."

There was a slight pause on the other end of the line. "Yes," she said. "I am too."

Damon cleared his throat. Why did this young girl make him feel so crazy inside? "I'd be happy to talk with you about your interest in the Brücke movement. I get the feeling you're enjoying Professor Heckman's art seminar."

"It's been *fascinating*," Lila said softly. "Professor Heckman has given me a whole new perspective on the period. But I'm glad he's bringing some new blood into the faculty."

"I'm new, all right," Damon said.

"Can you talk now?" Lila asked suddenly. "I can walk right over and meet you at your office."

Damon froze. Talk to her? Right now? He wasn't ready. He was exhausted. Wrung out. "My office hours are over now," he managed to say briskly. "But I'm free tomorrow night."

"Tomorrow night?" Lila said carefully, as if she wanted to make sure she heard him correctly.

"Sure," Damon said, trying to remind himself to slow down. He looked across at his cloud painting to calm himself but found that it only made his need to see Lila even more aching. "We could meet to talk about the Brücke over coffee . . . or maybe a drink . . . or dinner."

"Oh."

"Or whatever," Damon heard himself say, suddenly wondering if he'd gone too far. Lila, from what he could tell, was not exactly your typical American college girl. She looked older and more sophisticated than most of them. Maybe it was just the way she held herself that first time he saw her in class. The elegant cut of her clothes. Even the way she spoke. There was something special and refined about this girl. Something he couldn't quite put his finger on, but . . .

"I'd love to," Lila replied. "Do you want to meet somewhere downtown?"

"Sure," Damon said quickly, rousing himself. "Look. I'm not quite sure what time I'll be done with student conferences. Why don't we work out the details tomorrow?"

"Sure. Give me your number, and I'll call you."

"I can't," Damon said. "I don't have a home number. Let me call you. I'll give you a ring sometime tomorrow afternoon."

After hanging up, Damon put his hands flat down on the desk and kissed it. Then he sprang to his feet, raced to the picture, and kissed the face of the woman within it.

"Until tomorrow, Lila. Until tomorrow."

Chapter Three

"I loved your masked ball idea, Lila," Isabella enthused the following afternoon at Lila's apartment. She'd sunk her body deep into Lila's leather couch and was examining a spectacular piece of handblown glass she'd picked up from the coffee table. "Properly promoted, it could be the hottest thing on campus on alumni weekend."

"Thanks," Lila said, sipping an iced latte. She stared at the telephone, then looked irritably away. "Careful with that," she warned Isabella. "It's a Thomas Boulé original. Daddy bought it for me at a Christie's auction last month."

Isabella set it down, drew a brush out of her purse, and began drawing it through her long black hair. Like Lila, Isabella was slender and tanned, with a preference for simple yet elegant clothing and delicate gold jewelry. "I want to go as a fascinating gypsy princess."

"You're a fascinating gypsy princess already."

Isabella laughed and turned her head upside down, still brushing her hair. "I like the idea of going to a ball barefoot and covered with gold jewelry."

"Mmmm," Lila murmured. "The Thetas will make a fortune if we go with *that* idea." She checked her diamond-studded watch and walked over to the window.

"Oh, stop pacing, Lila," Isabella complained. "He'll call you."

"I *hate* this," Lila snapped.

"Hate what?" Isabella put away her brush and began flipping through a fashion magazine.

"I hate waiting."

Isabella raised one delicate eyebrow, her eyes not leaving the page. "The countess is not accustomed to being kept at bay."

"Well, you're right," Lila huffed. "I'm *not* used to it. I feel completely ridiculous being put in this position."

Lila glanced over, and her irritation worsened. Isabella was suppressing a smile.

"I can't believe I actually skipped my two o'clock class so that I wouldn't miss his call."

"Whew. The guy must be pretty amazing," Isabella said. "I mean, you *do* have a rather nice digital answering machine with every possible message-retrieving feature on the planet."

Lila chewed a nail. "I know."

"And *you* can't call *him*, right?" Isabella asked.

"I told you," Lila said irritably. "He said he didn't have a home number."

Isabella gave her a dry smile. "Oh. Right."

Lila hugged her stomach in frustration. The whole crazy attraction to Damon Price seemed to be fizzling in front of her eyes. "How could I have been so stupid? He sounded so strange when I asked him for his number. He *obviously* doesn't want me to call him."

"You've been out of circulation. . . ."

"Questions like that are needy and grasping," Lila interrupted. "I read *The Rules*. I know *The Rules*. Or at least I *used* to."

Isabella sighed.

"Of course, I *do* know his office number. . . ."

"But you said you thought he didn't want you to call."

"I *know*," Lila said. She covered her face with her hands and stood in the middle of her living room for a moment before sitting down opposite Isabella. She pointed a nearby remote control toward the far wall, and lush music began to pour out of her hidden speakers. "What am I doing?"

"You're brazenly pursuing a very good-looking TA," Isabella stated, slapping down her magazine and giving Lila a level stare. "But it's not just that

34

he's incredibly gorgeous," she began in a deadpan voice, repeating word for word what Lila had been telling her all morning. "You feel a strange affinity for him, as if you were meant to be with him."

Lila threw a pillow at her.

Isabella shrugged and continued her recitation. "It's like nothing you've ever felt before in your life for a complete stranger. You actually feel as if you've met him somewhere before." Isabella stopped. "How am I doing?"

Lila stared off, swaying to the music. "Don't worry. I know I sound like a complete fool."

"If you don't mind my saying so," Isabella said, fiddling with her charm bracelet, "I don't know why you're doing this either."

Lila looked down at her hands.

"What I mean is," Isabella began, sensing she had Lila's attention, "you don't *need* this guy— whoever he is."

Lila suddenly looked up. "What if he doesn't even *have* a phone?"

A look of alarm washed over Isabella's face.

Lila felt her eyes widen with panic. "What if he's one of those poverty-stricken doctoral candidates living in a seedy, run-down room with a phone down the hall?"

"And a *bathroom* down the hall," Isabella added with a knowing look.

Lila's eyes narrowed. She clicked off the music,

stood up, and began pacing across the silky Persian rug in front of her fireplace. "Maybe he knows something about me already—"

"Uh-huh," Isabella agreed with a nod. "Like how you are the widow of the Count di Mondicci and you're from a wealthy and prominent family yourself. You can never be too careful in your position, Lila."

Lila bit her lip and stared at Isabella in horror. "What have I done?"

"You don't *need* this guy," Isabella prompted her. "I mean, who is he?"

"He's a guy who can't even afford telephone service," Lila said slowly. "He's probably got bill collectors up to his ears—"

"And then he finds out about a beautiful, lonely young widow with millions to spare," Isabella finished her sentence. She paused and tilted her head thoughtfully to the side. "If he's a teacher, he's probably a lot older than you are. He might even be married."

Lila shivered and twisted the diamond pendant hanging at her throat. "Totally broke, with children's mouths to feed."

Isabella shook her head. "Besides, you've already got a boyfriend."

Lila nodded, remembering the touching letter and photo from Bruce. She felt a pang of guilt.

"Let's drive out to the beach and grab a pizza

at Julio's," Isabella suggested. "We've been here for hours. Come on. It's Friday."

Lila sprang up. "You're not kidding, it's Friday. Why am I sitting here, totally fixated on this jerk I don't even know . . . who has no phone . . . and is obviously after my money?"

Isabella grinned and grabbed her purse. "I have no idea. But let's get going."

But one moment later, as Lila was applying a new shade of lipstick in her bathroom and considering what dress to slip on, the cordless phone at her elbow rang.

Lila picked it up, every thought of Damon Price pushed completely out of her mind.

"Lila?"

"Yes?" Lila said absently, twisting down her lipstick and reaching for a brush.

"It's Damon."

For a second Lila just stood there, mute, as the sound of his voice seemed to take her back. To what, she didn't know.

"I'm free—finally. I'm calling about our plans for tonight."

Lila felt a wave of intense emotion wash over her. "Damon," she said quietly. "Oh, I'm so glad you called!"

In room 28, Dickenson Hall, Jessica lay stretched out on her rumpled bed. Romance novels, magazines, candy bar wrappers, and stray nail files littered the purple satin sheets. On the floor beside her were piles of discarded clothes and her twin sister Elizabeth's ab roller, which Jessica had tried for two minutes before giving up in disgust.

Jessica squirted another blob of Elizabeth's honey-rose body lotion on her leg. "Elizabeth isn't here to give me a lecture about not borrowing each other's favorite stuff," she muttered to herself. "Might as well take advantage."

Jessica rolled her eyes. Her Miss Superachiever twin sister, Elizabeth, was a reporter for WSVU, the college television station. She had managed to get herself a very cushy assignment helping a national TV network reporter cover the whale migration in Santa Barbara for five days.

And who did she ask to come along to stay at the fancy hotel and play on the beach? she wondered sarcastically. *Her own sister, Jessica? Of course not! She took her best friend, Nina Harper, Sweet Valley University's second-greatest superachiever and do-gooder.*

Jessica twisted the lotion cap shut and threw the bottle down on the bed, a smile beginning to form on her lips.

Then again, she mused, *maybe a freak hurricane is due to hit Santa Barbara. Stranger things have happened! I can just see her on a soggy beach, unable to get tape of a goldfish much less a whale migration.*

She plucked a bottle of new pink toenail polish from a department store bag sitting next to her bed and carefully separated her toes with bits of cotton. Heaving a huge sigh, she began dabbing her toenails, unable to believe that neither Lila nor Isabella had bothered to return her calls this afternoon.

She felt the beginning of tears. It was Friday night. She was between boyfriends. And she had absolutely no one to go out with. All she had to entertain her was the distant sound of flushing dorm toilets, the muted thuds of vintage hip-hop from the room above, and the partying shrieks gathered near the elevator down the hall.

That and the stupid wind lashing against my window, Jessica thought, jumping when the phone suddenly rang. She snatched up the cordless receiver hastily. "Hellooo?"

"Hi. It's me. Isabella."

Jessica made a face, cradled the phone under her chin, and curled over, continuing her pedicure. "Thanks for calling me back so fast."

She could hear Isabella give a frustrated sigh. "Sorry, Jessica. I've been over at Lila's."

Jessica huffed. "I left a message with her too. Are you both trying to ignore me?"

"She wouldn't have returned *Tom Cruise's* message, Jessica," Isabella explained. "She wanted the phone lines bare, undisturbed, and totally ready to ring."

"What?"

"Lila Fowler appears to have gone completely hot for her new art history TA," Isabella explained. "And before yesterday she'd never even talked to him."

Jessica felt her stomach turn into a hard ball. "And poor little Lila is already heartsick?"

"Lila spent the entire afternoon *waiting* for this guy to call her up and ask her out!"

"I'm sure," Jessica said through gritted teeth. "How could she humiliate herself like that?"

"I don't know," Isabella said. "But it *worked.*"

Jessica's eyes opened wide. "What do you mean, it *worked?*"

"She's with him now," Isabella said matter-of-factly. "They're on their first date as we speak."

Jessica resisted the urge to throw her new bottle of polish against the wall. "She told me that they kind of 'connected' in class. How did she swing this?"

"Connected?" Isabella cried. "All he did was look at her. Then he teased her because she dropped her purse and made a racket. Then she left him a message saying she wanted to see him."

Jessica was seriously stunned. "And he actually called her back?"

"Her strategy worked," Isabella said in her I-can't-believe-it-either voice. "He called her up while I was sitting there in her living room."

"She *talked* to him?"

"Of *course* she did," Isabella explained. "They

made plans for him to pick her up and take her to some little café near campus."

Jessica's heart sank again. "Oh."

"I know," Isabella soothed. "It's disgusting. She actually kicked me out so she could get ready. And from the totally frenzied look on her face, she probably tried on twenty outfits before she left with him."

"Poor Bruce," Jessica said lightly. "I mean, I could never understand her hopeless devotion to that jerk. But give me a break! Three days ago she told me that she and Bruce were 'destiny.'"

"I know," Isabella agreed. "It didn't take Lila long to forget him, did it?"

"Incredible."

"I guess."

Jessica bit her lip thoughtfully. "I mean, that is, if it's *true*."

"Of course it's true," Isabella objected. "She's head over heels."

Jessica shrugged. "Yeah. Unless she's been brainwashed or something."

"It's possible," Isabella said. "I can think of plenty of reasons why a poor, struggling TA like that would want to get close to Lila's millions."

Jessica made a sour face. "No kidding."

"I think I'll walk over to the house and see what's going on," Isabella said. "Want to come?"

Jessica stared at her unfinished toes and rolled her eyes. Friday night with the Thetas? She

41

wouldn't be caught dead looking like she didn't have anything better to do than sit around with her sorority sisters.

"Come on, Jessica."

"No, thanks. Actually something's just come up," Jessica lied. "Gotta go."

When Jessica finally hung up, she swallowed hard and fell back onto her pillow. Her room was dark and lonely. All she could think of was Lila, out with the mysterious art TA, just when she was formulating plans of her own to grab him for herself.

At the stoplight Damon smoothed his unruly hair down with both hands and strained to check himself out in the rearview mirror. He shook his head and fell back in his car seat. It was useless. Buried as he was under term papers, lecture notes, and classes, getting his hair cut had been the last thing on his mind. Now it fell forward into his eyes, sticking a little to his glasses.

You'll look like a bum next to her, he scolded himself. *What were you thinking when you asked her out?*

The light turned green, and Damon checked the slip of paper he'd used to scribble directions to Lila's place. "Left on Vine," he muttered. "Right on Orange. OK."

Leaves and branches scuttled across the dark road as Damon swung toward the curb and stopped. The place appeared to be surrounded by a stucco wall, laced with flowering vines and studded with a carved wooden gate entrance. *Lila doesn't exactly live in a bargain apartment complex for students,* he noted, scooping up the stray art magazines, research notebooks, and highlighter pens that littered the front of his car. He dumped them in the back and brushed off the passenger seat with his hand.

Finally Damon got out, slammed the car door, locked it, and smoothed the lapels of his corduroy jacket. The stiff breeze swayed the line of trees behind the wall. He stood up straight and walked up to the gate that led into the complex's enclosed courtyard.

"This is it," he said under his breath. "You got yourself into this, Price. And now you're going through with it."

Once inside, Damon could see what looked like six separate cottages surrounding a lush green lawn, each with a private porch and quaint wooden door. Tiny lanterns were positioned along the walkways, rocking gently in the wind. The spicy scent of jasmine was in the air.

"Hello, Damon."

He looked up, expecting to see the slender, slightly embarrassed college girl he'd glimpsed so briefly in class. Instead in the dim evening light he saw a woman in a close-fitting white dress standing still as a statue in the doorway. Her head was held high, and the wind was blowing her rich chestnut hair about her face, though she didn't seem to notice. Her deep-set eyes gave him a serene, direct look.

For a moment he wasn't even sure if it was the same girl. As he approached he saw that she was actually a stunningly beautiful woman. He drew closer, noticing the fine, pale texture of her skin, the lovely curve of her cheek, and the full lips that seemed to draw him in as he neared.

"Hello," Damon said, crunching forward on the gravel path. He wasn't exactly sure if he'd already greeted her out loud. It felt as if he'd been talking with her mentally even before they'd said a word. "You look wonderful."

"Thank you," she said, her lips spreading into a smile. She plucked a tiny jasmine blossom from the vine climbing her porch and smelled it. "Would you like to come in for a minute?"

"Sure," Damon said, walking ahead of her through the door of her cottage. "What a great old place," he said, admiring the shiny oak floors, coved ceilings, and archways. Above her wooden fireplace mantel was a stunning oil of a woman in a long dress reading a book under a tree.

"My father gave that to me as a housewarming gift when I got back from Europe," Lila said. "It's a Monmarche. Eighteen sixty-seven. He was a student of Manet's."

Damon raised his eyebrows and took a few

steps closer. "It must be incredibly valuable. Are you sure . . . I mean . . ."

Lila smiled shyly. "My father spoils me. It's true."

Damon cleared his throat, overwhelmed by the painting, by Lila, and by the feelings she stirred up in him. "You deserve to be spoiled," he said quietly, looking at her.

Lila's lips parted slightly, as if she were a little taken aback.

Damon bit his lip. "I'm sorry. I guess you just took my breath away. You look so beautiful in that dress and I—"

"You don't have to apologize," Lila assured him, lightly brushing a knuckle down the front of Damon's sleeve.

Damon felt a surge of electricity shoot through his body. "I think I do, actually. Here you are, looking so beautiful, and I'd only planned to take you to a little café out by the beach."

"It sounds wonderful," Lila said politely, her expression soft and eager.

Damon stared at the way her skin shone against the white straps of her dress. She looked like a silky flower standing there in her beautiful room. "You deserve something better. Something elegant, like—like dinner at Andre's," he tossed out casually. "But of course I can't . . ."

Lila's smile suddenly brightened. "Andre's? You know it?"

"Well, yes, and that's certainly where I'd take you if . . ."

Lila winked and turned away, picking up the cordless phone on the table next to her and quickly punching a phone number. She cupped her hand over the receiver. "Your wish is my command," she whispered.

Damon lifted a hand to protest, but Lila quickly turned away.

"Hello, this is Lila Fowler," Damon heard Lila murmur into the phone. "Is Andre available right now?"

Damon gulped.

"Andre? Lila Fowler. I'm fine. Yes, Daddy's great. He's in London right now on business. Listen. Will you have a table for two available in twenty minutes? You will?" Lila gushed. "Wonderful! See you then."

Lila hung up the phone and turned around, her face glowing and victorious. "Andre is saving us his best table."

Damon cleared his throat. "Lila, I hadn't planned on anything quite that fancy tonight. . . ."

He watched the light in Lila's delicate face begin to dim.

"What's wrong? You don't like the restaurant?" Lila asked.

"Well . . . yes," Damon stammered before he stopped trying altogether to explain. Andre's?

46

There was no way he could afford to take Lila to an expensive restaurant like that. He was a university teaching assistant, for Pete's sake, not an investment broker or a brain surgeon. But she looked so heartbreakingly beautiful standing there and . . . well . . . how could he say no?

"Would you rather not go?"

"No!" Damon said slowly, remembering the reimbursement check due from the university for his moving expenses. If he was lucky, it could be in his mailbox tomorrow morning. He could probably use some of that. Or ask for an advance on his first paycheck . . .

"Damon? Are you sure?"

"There's no place I'd rather go," Damon finally said with confidence. He reached out his hand for hers. "And you're coming with me, aren't you?"

"Yes," Lila said, taking his hand as they headed out the door and through the garden.

At her touch Damon felt dizzy yet solid at the same time. It was as if they were two pieces of a whole that suddenly fit together after a very, very long wait.

"I love these old Volkswagen Bugs."

Damon shifted down as they headed around a corner, the engine clattering like an eggbeater on metal. "You do?"

Actually Lila was telling the truth. She'd been driving around in BMWs, Mercedes, and Jaguars

47

so long, she'd forgotten what it was like to buzz around in a toy car like an ordinary college student. She leaned back and reached for the cute little strap that hung above the passenger window. It was fun driving around with nothing separating you from the world but a little bent steel and cracked glass. The experience was—well, it was clearing her head.

Lila laughed, leaned forward, and placed her palms on the tiny windshield in front of her. Then she walked her hands back across the low ceiling. "I love the way the car sort of scoops everyone together. . . ." She glanced over. Damon's face was inches away, and she flushed unexpectedly.

"It's cozy, all right," Damon agreed. He pulled onto a wide boulevard. "Am I heading the right direction? I think Andre's is on—"

"Camino Verde," Lila finished his sentence, pointing. "Turn right there."

Damon turned the steering wheel and gave her a nervous smile. "OK. How did you manage to swing a good table at Andre's at the last minute like that?"

Lila shrugged. "I'm a Fowler."

His smile relaxed a little. "What does that mean, Ms. Fowler?"

"Where are you from, Damon?"

He rubbed the back of his neck. "Born and raised in Connecticut, actually. But we Prices still had to make advance reservations when we went out to dinner."

48

"Mmmm," Lila teased back. "Well, here in Sweet Valley we Fowlers have a reputation for wanting and enjoying the very best that life has to offer. And we don't like to wait for it."

"I see that."

Lila laughed. "Actually my family's been going to Andre's for special occasions ever since I can remember. So Andre likes to pamper the charming little daughter, I guess."

"The guy has great business sense."

Lila caught his eye with her smile, but Damon quickly looked away and cleared his voice uncomfortably. Lila's heart sank. Had she said something wrong? "Is—is everything OK?"

Damon stretched his arm out on the steering wheel and tucked in his chin, as if he were bracing himself to say something. "Lila. I feel really bad about this, but the only reason I was taking you to a little café instead of Andre's is that . . . well, the café is a little more in my price range. I'll be honest with you; I don't—"

Lila impulsively turned in her seat, touched by his honesty. "Please," she interrupted, "you don't have to explain. I—I shouldn't have called for that table. I feel so stupid."

"Hey. I should have said something earlier."

Lila bit her lip. "Look. It's all my fault. Let me pick up the tab this time."

Did I just say that? Lila thought in a panic. *Did*

49

*I, Lila Fowler, actually wait all afternoon for a guy
to call me, climb into his junk heap of a car, then tell
him I would pay for dinner?*

Trembling with confusion, Lila pointed at the familiar gold-and-white awning fluttering ahead. A
valet stood at attention as Damon swung his tiny car
into the U-shaped drive and stopped in front of the
awning, where the valet briskly opened Lila's door.

Damon didn't move. "You don't have to do
this, Lila. The little beach café has great burgers."

Lila smiled shyly. "This will be fun. Let me pay
just this once. Really."

*You've never done anything like this before in
your life,* Lila's mind screamed at her. *What's gotten into you?*

"OK, then," Damon said. He reached over and
lightly touched her bare shoulder, sending a current of warmth all the way down to her fingertips.
The valet had already opened her car door, and
she knew that she should get up off the seat. But
now she could barely get her legs to move.

That's what's gotten into me, Lila thought, finally stepping out of the car, straightening, and
heading toward the restaurant's shiny wood door
with Damon at her side.

Chapter Four

"May I bring you a drink or an appetizer while you look at your menus?" the waiter asked.

"I'll have a glass of burgundy," Damon said.

Lila was beaming at him from across the white tablecloth. "Do you have the *petits chaussons au* Roquefort tonight?"

"Yes, we do, Miss Fowler."

"I'll have those, please," Lila said, leaning toward Damon and crossing her arms on the edge of the table. "You'll love them."

Damon looked around the room. The maitre d' had given them an intimate table that was set in a round alcove of the restaurant overlooking a spectacular garden that stirred in the breeze. Each table had fresh flowers, and classical music flowed from hidden speakers.

"I could get used to this," Damon told her.

He took off his jacket as he started to relax. Then he let out a laugh and clasped his hands in front of him on the table.

"Mmmm," Lila hummed, sipping ice water.

"So. You want to talk about art."

He sensed the brightness in her eyes dimming a little. "Oh. Yes. Um . . ."

"The Brücke." Damon worked to keep a straight face. "Come on, Lila. You said you'd seen the works of the Brücke movement in Europe and you wanted to discuss your research . . . on Claude Monet."

"Yes," Lila replied, a smile forming in the corner of her mouth as the waiter set down a basket of bread and Damon's glass of wine. "For class."

"For class."

"Mmmm." Lila smiled down at her water glass.

Damon smiled at her. "Monet was an impressionist, Lila. Not an expressionist."

Lila bit her lip. "Um. Yes. But wasn't he influenced by the expressionists?"

Damon shook his head slowly, the smile not leaving his face. "We don't have to talk about art if you don't want to." He wasn't sure if his feelings were taking him where she wanted him to go. But what was happening between him and Lila had nothing at all to do with the Brücke movement, expressionism, or even art for that matter. He was pretty sure of that.

"Maybe we should talk about art after dinner,"

Lila suggested. She glanced down at the menu. "After our filet of beef stuffed with foie gras and truffles, for instance?"

"You recommend it?"

Lila gazed into his eyes. "Yes, I do."

A gust of wind rumbled against the window and the candlelight flickered, sending light and shadow over Lila's lovely face as she ordered. Damon sipped his wine and breathed in the fragrance of the flowers and the good food that surrounded them. He was beginning to wonder if he'd ever felt so relaxed and happy with another person in his entire life.

"Tell me about yourself, Lila Fowler," Damon finally asked after they were served their dinner.

"I grew up here in Sweet Valley," Lila said, "but moved to Italy before I started college. That's where I met my husband, Tisiano."

Damon's eyes grew wide. He gulped back a sip of his wine and set down the glass, stunned. A cold dread spread all over his body. She couldn't be married. There was no way. . . .

"Tisiano was killed in a Jet Ski accident only a few months after we were married," Lila said quietly.

Damon sat back in his chair with relief. He realized that he'd begun to break out in a cold sweat, and as he wiped his palms on the tops of his pant legs he wondered guiltily if he'd ever felt so happy about another human being's untimely death.

53

"Sometimes I miss him very much," Lila said with sadness. "Yet there are other times when I realize how different we were."

Damon slid his hand across the table, dizzy with relief. He touched her wrist with his fingertips. "Tell me how you were different."

Lila's eyes grew misty. "He was much older than I was, for one." She pushed her plate away a little and settled her slender elbows on the edge of the table. "Maybe not that much older in years, but older in . . . experience. He was a businessman."

"What kind of business?"

Lila shrugged. "Family business, computers. The di Mondicci family has holdings all over the world, and he managed everything. His title was Count di Mondicci."

Count di Mondicci? Damon asked himself, startled. *I'm on a date with the widow of some Italian count? What am I doing here? Who do I think I am? How can I possibly compete?*

Damon watched as tears began to pool in Lila's large brown eyes. She lifted her white napkin up to her face. "I never really felt at home in Italy. I wanted to come home right away after his death. So I've been here at school ever since."

The conversation had taken on a new seriousness, but it was clear Lila didn't want to dwell on her problems.

"Let's talk about you," she said slowly, lifting her

54

eyes to his. They were a little shiny and pink around the rims now, making her look more beautiful and vulnerable. Damon wanted to sit there forever, looking into her eyes, not saying anything at all. For some crazy reason it didn't seem necessary. It was as if they'd been together for a very long time, and though they'd only just begun to share the ordinary, surface facts of their lives, the deeper undercurrents had already been exchanged and understood.

"Will there be anything else, sir?"

Damon broke his lock on Lila's eyes. How long had they been sitting there together, not speaking? Five minutes? An hour?

"Dessert, perhaps? Coffee?"

Damon's eyes searched Lila's again, and he knew the answer immediately. Slowly, hesitantly, he slid his hand across the tablecloth and took Lila's. "No, thank you. We'll need the check now, please."

The night is just beginning, isn't it, Lila? he asked silently. *Just beginning.*

Outside Andre's the wind was stirring in the trees and the air smelled of salt and eucalyptus. Damon slipped his arm lightly around Lila's shoulders.

"Cold?"

Lila shook her head.

Damon handed the valet the keys to the Volkswagen, and as they waited they silently watched the dark clouds marching across the sky, every few moments revealing a field of brilliant stars.

Suddenly they both looked at each other and nodded. *"Starry, starry night,"* they sang together, laughing.

"I've got such a soft spot in my heart for van Gogh," Damon confessed.

"I saw that painting at the National Gallery in London," Lila told him. "I think I sat there and looked at it for an hour. Everyone in the tour thought I was crazy."

Damon's mouth had dropped open slightly in disbelief. "I did too. Just a week or two ago. I *love* that painting. It's so much richer and luminescent when you see the real thing—"

"Right in front of you, yes," Lila said, finishing his sentence, then stopping and looking away. She prayed he didn't notice the color creeping into her cheeks.

The Volkswagen was whisked in front of them.

"Would you like to stop by my place for coffee before I take you home?" Damon asked over the rumbling of the engine.

Lila felt a shudder of excitement. She climbed into the passenger seat after the valet opened the squeaky door for her. "Yes, I would."

"It's just a little place near campus," Damon was saying. He smiled, and his smile was so wide and white in his tanned face, Lila thought she would faint. "Actually it's not an apartment. It was originally the carriage house for a large estate."

Lila nodded, and as Damon continued to drive she sneaked a quick look at his profile and bit her lip. Could Isabella be right? Was it possible that he was interested in her because of her money? She let her head fall back onto the headrest. She certainly hadn't made any secret of it, but when she was around Damon, she couldn't help being completely open and honest. What was she supposed to do? Lie?

Of course, I did pay for dinner, Lila thought worriedly.

Finally Damon pulled into a gravel driveway that led behind an enormous mansion. "This big old place is used for alumni functions and housing for people attending workshops. Stuff like that."

Lila peered ahead. A little craftsman-style cottage stood at the end of the path, lit from the inside by a small lamp in the window. "It's darling," she said.

"Come on in," Damon said shyly. He hopped out of the car, walked around it, and opened the door for her.

Lila stepped over the gravel. Her white dress blew whispering around her legs, and up above, the mounting wind was howling in the trees surrounding the house. Damon put the key in his front door and pushed it open. Standing at the threshold, she stared inside as Damon walked ahead and turned on lamps scattered throughout the big living room.

"It's a wonderful place, Damon," Lila said. She laughed, then she looked around the room. A brick fireplace acted as the centerpiece, with large, floor-to-ceiling bookcases on each side. On the opposite side of the room were more tall bookshelves with a wooden ladder leaning against them. There was a large, slipcovered couch facing the fireplace, illuminated by a lovely stained glass lamp on a side table. Beautifully framed posters from art exhibits around the world hung neatly on the walls.

"You made your place sound like a tiny little apartment," Lila said shyly, walking inside.

Damon put his hands on his hips and looked around, nodding. "It's pretty nice, isn't it? Professor Heckman helped me get it. It's small, actually. But I've finally got room for some of the things I've collected along the way."

Lila walked forward, her hand trailing along the couch's silky fabric with relief. He certainly didn't *seem* like a down-and-out academic who was out to take advantage of her. Near the window at the end of the room was a massive oak rolltop desk that had been opened to reveal stacks of books and papers, a computer, a thick Rolodex file, and a . . .

A telephone? Lila's mind raced. For a moment she just stood there, staring at it. Then she turned around slowly and looked at Damon, who was flipping eagerly through what looked like a large album of photographs.

"Damon," Lila said slowly.

"Yeah?" His flipping slowed and a big grin

spread across his face, as if he'd found what he was looking for.

Lila felt her face harden. Was he trying to hide something from her? "I thought you said you didn't have a phone."

Damon looked confused. "I didn't have a . . . what?" He looked back down at the album and gestured eagerly for her to take a look. "There's something I want to show you."

"You said you didn't have a telephone," Lila interrupted, her voice cold.

Damon looked up and frowned.

"A phone," Lila insisted. "Yesterday you told me you didn't have a phone."

"I *didn't* have a phone yesterday," Damon said, as if she'd asked a strange question. He motioned for her to sit next to him. "It was just installed this morning. Look. Proof. Here I am standing in front of the National Gallery, still reeling from the van Gogh exhibit."

Lila sat down and studied Damon's profile as he turned the pages. They were sitting so close now that she could smell his spicy aftershave and feel the warmth of his leg so near to hers. His hands, long and tapered, moved across the page as he talked about his travels and the friends he'd met.

She took him in as she had taken in the room, barely listening to his words. All she could think of was the image she had in her mind—that she was standing at the edge of a cliff and that she was about to leap off into the unknown.

Damon Price. What did she know about him except that he filled her with a mysterious longing that made her heart beat harder and her face flush hot? And why exactly did she feel that way about him?

Lila closed her eyes. It had been almost the same with Tisiano. She'd taken a big risk falling for him and marrying him the way she did, so impulsively. And she'd been left with a huge hole in her heart when he was gone.

Sometimes she thought that was why she had settled for Bruce Patman: handsome, rich, completely devoted to her, and—well—*predictable*. For the first time she began to ask herself whether that was what she really wanted.

Lila stared at the slick of Damon's tanned skin and the way his eyes gleamed at her. Just one look and she knew that nothing was predictable or safe with Damon.

But then again, love is always dangerous, she told herself. *The only question is, am I ready to risk it?*

"I'm sorry I keep going on about my travels," Damon said. "It was just a very intense time for me."

Lila leaned her head back on the couch. "Traveling is intense. I think it's partly because you learn about yourself when you're in an unfamiliar place."

Damon leaned back too, then turned his head so that their faces were level. "And what did you learn, Lila," he whispered, drawing near, his expression tender, "when you were away from home for so long?"

Lila felt her breath rushing out of her body in one quick puff, as if she'd been caught off guard by the closeness of him. She touched his shoulder as he drew closer. "I learned," she said softly, "to open my mind. And to trust my instincts."

"And what do your instincts tell you now?" Damon whispered, cupping her cheek in one hand.

Damon's face moved toward hers. Lila closed her eyes, then opened them when she felt his hands tracing the outline of her face, her lips, the line of her jaw. She let her head fall back as Damon began to kiss her.

It was a kiss she wanted to replay in her head a hundred times instantly. Her face at a slight angle to his. The softness of his lips, gentle at first, then firmer, then melting into hers until she lost track of time. It was a long, soft first kiss that made her feel dizzy and secure all at the same time.

Lila stroked the side of his face with one hand. "My instincts tell me not to be afraid."

Damon ran his fingers through Lila's thick, soft hair, then bent down to kiss her again. His body was burning, but his mind was quiet and sure. He knew this woman. He belonged to her in some strange and special way that he had no desire to analyze. His feelings for her were just there, like the air he breathed.

He pulled away and looked down at her, smiling. Her hair was spread out on the back of the couch like a crown, and her eyes were full of yearning. Gently he took her hand and pulled her down so that she was lying next to him on the soft couch. His arms wrapped tightly around her slender body, taking in the feel of her. The curves of her body seemed to meld into his. They felt like two lost halves of the same whole, finally brought together after a long journey.

"I can't believe this is happening," Lila whispered. Her eyes were damp and shining. "I mean, I never thought that something like this could happen so fast."

Damon wrapped his arms tighter around Lila and let out a long, happy sigh. "I don't know how to put it into words right now, but I feel as if I've known you for a long time."

Lila nodded. "It's strange, isn't it?" She laughed softly. "I mean, I could probably tell you right now what your favorite colors are. Your favorite food . . ."

Damon smiled at the same time she did, and together they nodded. "Filet of beef stuffed with foie gras and truffles," they said in unison, laughing.

Lila's face turned serious. "Maybe we *have* met."

Damon stroked her cheek and gazed into her eyes. Outside, the wind howled in the trees and branches scraped against the side of the house. "Believe me, Lila. I would remember if we had."

Lila kissed the hollow of his neck, and Damon felt as if his body were on fire. "I would have remembered too. Still, everything about you seems so familiar. Your face. Your voice . . ."

"I feel," Damon said fiercely, "that I could lie here with you all night and . . ."

Lila began to laugh softly, kissing his neck. "Never want to leave?"

Damon nodded, sighing. "When I'm with you, it's the strangest thing. I feel as if I belong to you. As if I'm floating on a cloud, where there's no need, no problems, no friction . . ."

Something clicked in Damon's mind that made him stop talking.

"What?" Lila murmured.

The cloud picture, Damon thought. *The woman in the clouds.*

"I need to show you something," Damon said, sliding away from Lila and standing up. He rubbed his jaw and scanned his bookshelves. "A painting."

"Why, Damon?" Lila asked, propping herself up on one elbow.

Damon's heart speeded up. "You'll see what I mean."

He got up from the couch, impatient to show her. But he had forgotten where he'd placed the book. A large one. White dust jacket with black lettering. Damon paced back and forth in front of the bookshelves, scanning the titles. It had been a volume on the surrealists he'd bought as an undergraduate. It was in tatters by the time he'd finished his master's degree.

"May I help?" Lila asked, slipping off the couch and following him. "What is it you're looking for?"

"It's a picture, Lila," Damon said earnestly, taking hold of the ladder as he spotted the spine of the familiar book, shelved high on the wall. "I've got to show it to you. It's—it's just really important."

"OK."

Damon's heart was pounding now. His feelings for Lila seemed to be so mysteriously tied up with his passion for the cloud painting, he had to see it again. He knew in his heart that it was her face within the clouds of the painting. But somehow he needed Lila to see it to make it real. To make it real for both of them.

"Lila," Damon asked, "would you hold the bottom of this ladder while I climb up? I'm not sure how stable it is."

"Sure."

He began climbing the ladder toward the book, which was lodged on the right-hand side of the top shelf, near the ceiling. "What picture do you want me to see?" Lila asked. "Tell me."

"Just a minute," Damon called down, scanning the book titles as he climbed higher. *Metropolitan*

Seminars in Art, The Art of Pieter Brueghel, Romantic Poetry and Prose. Each one was connected to a memory and a place.

When Damon reached the top rung of the ladder, the book he wanted was just within his reach, and he grasped the top of the spine to wedge it out of its place on the shelf. The heavy book leaned outward, and Damon spread his fingers to catch it. His hand, however, wasn't prepared for the expected heft of the book. It came out of the shelf into his hand, but its weight bent his hand backward against his wrist until it became impossible to hold.

"Lila!" he warned as he felt the book slipping backward over his arm. "Lila, look out!"

The book flipped backward and sailed down through the air, headed for the bare wood of the floor. But at the last second Lila leaned out to look up at him, placing her head in the line of fire.

"What—" she began to reply just as the corner of the book caught her head at full force, sending her crashing to the floor.

"Lila!" Damon screamed, scrambling down the ladder. He stared in horror at her slight body, which lay crumpled on the floor, still and deathly pale.

At first Lila saw only darkness. She tried to move and felt a piercing pain on the side of her head and in her shoulder. She struggled to open her eyes and saw the blurry outline of a chair leg.

She felt scratchy carpeting on her cheek, then a firm hand slipping under her head.

When her vision cleared, she was lying in Damon's arms, staring up into his dark green eyes, which were now filled with fear. She started to speak, but a stabbing pain tore through her head, forcing her to close her eyes against the light.

"Lila? Can you hear me?" Damon whispered.

She parted her lips to speak but could manage only a low moan. Her mouth, dry and slow, didn't work. And her head cracked with pain with every beat of her heart.

"Are you OK?" His voice sounded frightened to her.

She struggled to sit up.

"I'm so sorry," Damon murmured. "The book just slipped right out of my hand."

Lila put her hand on her forehead. "I'm OK." She gulped. "Really."

"Come on, let's get you up to the couch," Damon said, helping her to her feet. "Oh, I'm so sorry."

"Thank you," Lila whispered, setting her head down on a pillow. The pain in her head had subsided, but her limbs felt heavy and her stomach felt sick.

"Is—is there anything I can get you?" Damon asked, his voice desperate.

She closed her eyes and opened them again. She saw his face in a blurry haze, wearing an expression so tender and caring, she could barely bring herself to tell him what she wanted. But she wanted to go home.

For a moment Damon was quiet, searching her eyes with his until he squeezed her hand in his and softly kissed her cheek. "I'm going to take you home, Lila. Just let me watch you for a few minutes to make sure you're OK. I don't want you to fall asleep alone with a concussion."

Lila nodded sadly. Yet she was grateful that he understood the spell had been broken. She needed to go home, and Damon was sensitive enough to figure that out.

He was, she thought, probably the first man who would ever truly understand her needs.

Even if he *had* just knocked her out cold.

Chapter Five

"Everything is so beautiful!"
"Congratulations!"
"Wonderful party!"

As the people called out to her she was walking across a lush lawn bordered by flower gardens and dotted with white tables and chairs. In the distance she could see a band playing on the wide terrace that led to the base of an enormous stone mansion. Yellow-and-white-striped awnings fluttered nearby while waiters in black tie moved noiselessly about, serving champagne and silver platters of hors d'oeuvres.

To her right the wide blue ocean beckoned, and the sapphire sky was dotted with pure white clouds.

She breathed in the scent of lilac and roses and, looking down, realized that she was carrying a bouquet of them and that a filmy white veil was blowing gently about her face.

"Flora!"

She turned around and watched as a woman hurried toward her, holding her hat and tiny veil in place with one hand. She smiled, noting the woman's slim-fitting suit, pinched in tightly at the waist and falling nearly to her ankles, where it was met with a pair of chunky pumps.

"Congratulations, darling!" the woman cried, taking her upper arms and kissing her stiffly on each cheek before pulling back. "You look fabulous!"

She looked down and saw that her own dress was a tailored sheath made of white silk that spilled to the ground. In a glance she could see that it was embroidered all over with thousands of tiny white pearls. She was the bride, the guests were her friends, and that huge mansion sailing against the blue sky was her new home.

"Where's that handsome husband of yours, Flora?" the woman cried gaily. She turned to the side and began waving someone over. "Theodore! There you are!"

In slow motion she turned toward her new husband, who was moving eagerly toward her. He was wearing his black tuxedo suit over an immaculately starched white shirt and black tie, setting off his tawny skin. His hair, parted near the middle, was combed back behind his high forehead, and his large green eyes glimmered as he approached.

"Theodore," she murmured as he took her left hand in his and kissed it tenderly. There was a large sparkling ring on her fourth finger, and she gazed proudly at the cluster of emeralds surrounding the massive single diamond that dominated the center. Together they looked at the ring again. "It's so lovely, Theodore."

"I'd say the hand," Theodore replied, leaning down once again and kissing her fingertips.

"We should greet our guests," she heard herself say. She felt a surge of love and happiness, as if all the ordinary cares of the world had lifted this one day just to celebrate their union. The ground itself felt soft as a cloud.

"Flora! Theodore!" two couples cried out, hurrying down the lawn, champagne glasses in hand.

One of the women, whose tight blond curls lay plastered against the side of her rosebud mouth, was laughing as the group came to a stop. "James and Mooky just jumped in your lovely fountain to cool off, Theo. This party is absolutely *wild!*"

The man, also wearing a tuxedo, shook her hand. "It's so lovely to see you two together as man and wife. Incredible what true love can inspire, isn't it?" he asked, gesturing toward the lavish party at the top of the slope.

"It's the wedding of the decade," the second woman announced, sticking her long cigarette holder delicately between her lips and puffing. "Why else do you think Eddie and I jumped that train from San Francisco to come?"

"Clive and Dorothy were in Europe when they heard about the big day," the man chimed in. "They immediately hopped a steamer to New York."

"When are you going to paint your bride's portrait, Theodore?" another voice called out gaily.

Theodore raised his hand in laughing protest. "All in good time, my friends. She'll be my most precious subject."

Flora smiled and leaned her head on Theodore's shoulder.

"Stop!" the woman with the cigarette cried out. She waved frantically to the wedding photographer, who was setting up a tripod and camera near them on the lawn. "Theo, Flora, you absolutely *have* to have your picture taken right there, just like that."

Theodore nudged her. "What do you say, Flora?"

She smiled and straightened, smoothing down her hair. "Of course. But let me have a few minutes with my face."

Theodore kissed her, and she floated up the groomed lawn to the terrace, then through the crush of bobbing, dancing, congratulating guests until she was inside a huge pair of French doors. She looked up. It was a large, cool room with soaring ceilings, tall windows, and tasteful arrangements

71

of gilt furniture among the carpets and stately interior columns. The party's lighthearted music still hung in the air, but it was faint now as she headed toward the vast sweep of staircase leading to the second floor, where her room must surely be.

She stopped, feeling the swoosh of her hem on the polished floor. The white walls of the room were hung with the most unusual and striking pictures she'd ever seen.

She narrowed her eyes and turned. At the far end of the room was a huge, mural-size painting of amoeba-shaped objects, each one filled with a different bright color and outlined with thick, black brush strokes. On the adjoining wall was an eerie landscape of angels bursting from trees and lion heads emerging from cliffs of stone.

She began walking up the stairs, taking note of an even stranger painting that hung on the curve of the ascending wall. The picture was of a blue ocean that curved away to the horizon, where it was met with a violet sky. As she looked at the horizon she began to see a pattern in the texture of the water, which finally revealed the outline of a beautiful angel.

Fascinated and mystified, she continued floating up the stairs until she reached a gold-painted double door, which opened magically, as if it were expecting her arrival. Inside the bedroom a lavish mirrored vanity awaited her, set with silver-backed hairbrushes and ivory combs.

She sat down and saw her slender reflection in the mirror. Carefully she slipped off her veil, laid it aside, and primped her thick chestnut hair, which was short and carefully waved so that it rippled artfully along the lines of her cheekbones, where it fell just short of her glossy, red-painted lips.

She dabbed her nose with powder from the mother-of-pearl compact set before her. Her porcelain skin glowed with happiness. When she was finished, she fastened the veil back onto her head and stood up, smoothing down the drape of her shimmering gown.

Theodore and I have each other for always, she thought. *This is the happiest day of my life.*

"Flora," she heard Theodore calling in the distance.

"I'm coming, dear," she whispered, fluffing out her veil and floating out of the room toward the staircase.

"You look so beautiful today," Theodore said as he stood at the bottom of the stairs. "Like an angel swinging from a cloud."

"Our cloud," she murmured back, hurrying down the stairs, feeling her veil flutter around her face. She reached out her hands to join his, which were now outstretched. But as she did she felt her right foot catch on the thick carpeting beneath her slipper.

Her head began to drop, the stairway began to fall away, and she felt herself pitching forward into darkness. She was falling—falling straight through into a spinning void, her wedding veil swirling maddeningly about her face in the deep, deep darkness.

"No!" Lila cried out, sitting straight up in bed, frantically scattering the dream veil away from her face.

After a moment she looked around her room. There was the solid bed beneath her. The familiar walls and furniture. Her own body, shivering in the morning light. She glanced at her digital clock. Seven-thirty, Wednesday morning.

Lila fell back into her feather pillow, clasping her forehead with one hand. "Damon?"

She closed her eyes in frustration. Ever since her date with Damon on Friday night, her nights had been tossed with dreams of him. Images of his face emerging from cloud. The outline of his back disappearing into a crowd.

But this dream had been different. This dream had been so lifelike, Lila was sure she could still smell the roses and lilacs from her wedding bouquet. Even stranger, Lila had the strong feeling that she'd actually been to the sumptuous mansion before, long ago. In her mind she traveled again through its rooms, trying in vain to remember. Was it a childhood memory or a repeat of a dream she'd had before and forgotten?

Lila slipped out of bed and wandered into the living room. She bit her lip. Just thinking about Damon made her shiver. But thinking about a wedding between her and Damon was like diving into even more dangerous waters. The wedding seemed too real to her. She could taste the cold champagne in her mouth and hear the band playing distantly in her ears.

Lila's head was spinning. She could feel herself melt under the heat of Damon's green eyes in the dream. But why had he been called Theodore? Why had everyone called her Flora? For that matter, why had the clothes been so odd? The last time she'd seen anyone wearing a veiled hat was in the cathedrals of Florence. And why were her wedding guests talking about steamers? Hadn't anyone thought of catching a plane?

She headed toward the bathroom. Professor Heckman's art seminar would be starting in an hour, and she knew Damon would be lecturing. She had to wake up, get dressed, and think of something intelligent to say about the surrealists.

Staring into the mirror, Lila touched her face. The face from her dream but without the white veil and the rosy glow. She hugged her stomach and breathed in deeply, trying to calm herself. The dream had brought her so achingly close to Damon that the fact he hadn't called her since Saturday became even more painful.

"Why haven't you called, Damon?" Lila whispered. She drew a comb slowly through her hair and tied it back with a clip. Damon had called her later the night of her accident to make sure she was OK, but since then her phone had been silent.

Had he forgotten about her? Had the night been a disappointment to him?

Lila turned on the faucet and splashed her face with cold water, determined to shake off her negative thoughts. It was true she hadn't spoken to Damon in four days. It was true that she was nervous about seeing him again in class. But then, Damon wasn't a kid in college. He was a busy TA and doctoral candidate, teaching four classes and spending most of his nights grading papers. He would call when the time was right.

She was sure of it. The dream, in its own way, had foretold it.

She and Damon were meant to be together.

Chapter Six

"OK, Price," Damon muttered, "it's show time. Time to turn up the energy."

Damon slipped on his glasses and held a color slide of a famous surrealist painting up to the light before putting it in the slide projector. Reaching over to the lectern, he grabbed his takeout latte and gulped it. He'd been up until the early morning hours grading freshman papers, which had left him groggy and not particularly prepared for this morning's lecture.

The lecture hall was empty for now, and a thick morning fog pressed against the windows.

"Salvador Dalí. Right," he muttered to himself, slipping another slide into the projector. "OK. Follow that up with Max Ernst."

Damon slipped the last slide in and snapped the top shut. He couldn't remember the last time he'd felt so exhausted. The morning after his date with Lila, Professor Heckman had telephoned him, insisting that he come to a weekend seminar he was conducting at a famous university three hours away.

Damon shifted his eyes to the lecture hall entrance at the top of the aisle, wondering whether he would ever see Lila again. First he knocked her out cold at his apartment. Then he left town suddenly and didn't see her at all over the weekend.

He rubbed his eyes with both hands, then stared absently at the empty doorway. When he'd returned to Sweet Valley on Monday morning, he was inundated with work and phone calls. And he had to admit, in the back of his mind, he was convinced he'd blown it with Lila. Maybe he really hadn't had the courage to call her.

So here I stand, waiting for her, he thought. *Waiting for her reaction. Waiting and hoping like a helpless jerk. Why didn't I just call her? Why couldn't I take the chance?*

Damon opened his notebook and tried to focus his thoughts. Still, the image of Lila's face haunted him, as it had for the past four days. It was a feeling he wasn't used to. He'd had girlfriends before, maybe even been in love. But he'd never been drawn to a woman so quickly or intensely. He'd never had the feeling before that he belonged—*really* belonged—to someone like that.

Damon clenched his jaw in frustration. Was it

78

overwhelming fear that had kept him from her? Was he such a coward after all?

"Damon?"

With a shock Damon realized that the voice belonged to Lila, and as he looked up he saw that she was descending the amphitheater stairs toward him. He gulped. Just looking at her made his heart ache. The smooth skin of her arms shone against the white of her sleeveless blouse, and her chestnut hair, even in the semidarkness, seemed to light up the air around her.

"Lila," Damon murmured, stepping forward around to the front of the lectern.

She seemed embarrassed. Her usual smart confidence had been replaced with a pale, timid expression. Slowly she moved toward him, hugging her notebooks close to her chest. "I'm sorry I'm a little early," she said softly, her brown eyes lifting toward his. "I just wanted to say hello."

Damon searched her eyes. "You probably hate me."

Her face seemed suddenly to flush as she neared, and he could see from her cautious expression that she was unsure what to say next.

"I—I don't know what to say," Damon continued in a rush. He held his hands out a little as he tried to think of a way to apologize. "I'm so sorry I haven't called."

Her brown eyes seemed to mist over. "It's OK; I didn't—"

"No, no, no," Damon interrupted, waving her words away, "you don't understand. Professor Heckman had me attend a seminar over the weekend unexpectedly, and I got back late . . . and when I returned, I felt so bad. . . . I didn't call because . . . I was afraid of . . ."

Her face seemed to light up, and a small curve of a smile began to form in the corner of her mouth. "Afraid?" she said softly, stepping forward and lowering her clutch of notebooks. "Afraid of what?"

Damon sighed. "I don't know. I guess I was too afraid of your reaction. First I hurt you when I dropped that book on your head, and then I had to leave town suddenly. Everything seemed to be working against us."

"No, Damon," Lila protested. She placed a slender hand on his arm. "It's OK."

"I should have called you, but . . ."

"But what?"

Damon looked up. "I was afraid you'd never want to see me again," he blurted.

"What?"

Damon raked back his hair. "I don't know what came over me. I don't understand it."

Her eyes seemed to narrow. She nodded slowly, as if she understood what he was saying. "I don't understand what's happening between us either. But it's not something we can ignore, is it?"

"Lila," Damon breathed, reaching for her.

She set her notebooks down in the aisle, turned, and slipped her arms around his neck. Then she pressed her cheek against his chest. "I need to be able to trust you."

Damon felt his heart cracking in two. "I've been so thoughtless. So afraid to risk anything."

Lila lifted her face to his, and Damon bent down to kiss her. Suddenly, magically, his hands were in her hair, her lips were on his neck, his face, his mouth. "I'm willing to take that risk," she whispered finally, pulling away.

Damon had bent down again to her face, enveloping her body with his arms, when he heard a sound at the top of the amphitheater. He froze, still clinging to Lila, as a curt woman's voice cut through the silence.

"*Excuse* me. May I sit down?"

Jessica stood at the door to the lecture hall, staring with fascination at the view in front of her. There, for everyone in the world to see, was poor, lonely Lila Fowler, glued to the chest of the best-looking guy Jessica had seen all year on the Sweet Valley University campus.

She had the craziest urge to burst out laughing, but she held back and went for the angry, shocked approach instead, which worked beautifully. What fun it was to see Lila pull away from handsome Art Boy! How completely entertaining

81

it was to see both of their scared faces looking up at her!

"Jessica?" Lila said, sweeping her hair off her face with an impatient gesture.

"Oh, Lila!" Jessica called out, hurrying forward. "Is that *you*?"

Lila's glare seemed to bore holes through the air.

Jessica sauntered boldly forward, her gaze shifting from Lila's angry face to Art Boy's. Then Jessica's mind snapped off. The guy was tall, tawny skinned, and almost movie star handsome. She took in his endearingly rumpled brown hair; his deep green, intelligent eyes; full lips; and muscular jawline. Lila was on to something.

And Lila was definitely not free like Jessica was.

"Is this a friend of yours, Lila?" he asked in an irritated voice. His eyebrows were narrowed in anger.

"Yes, I *am* Lila's friend," Jessica came back without missing a beat. "Probably her *best* friend."

Lila's face flushed an angry red. "Damon, this is Jessica Wakefield."

Jessica gave Damon her most brilliant smile, trying to ignore the wobbly feeling in her knees. "Hi, Damon. *So* pleased to meet you."

"Hello," he replied in a stern voice.

"Damon is Professor Heckman's new teaching assistant for the class," Lila explained, reaching reluctantly for her notebooks on a nearby chair.

Jessica ignored Lila's glare and let her eyes zoom

in on Damon. "I'm one of Professor Heckman's students, and I *love* this lecture." She checked her watch, sat down in the nearest seat, and crossed her legs. "Guess that's why I'm a little early."

"Really?" Damon said curtly.

Jessica nodded. "Yes," she said, letting her eyes open wide, as if she'd just had a wonderful thought. "Lila. You'll *have* to introduce Damon to Bruce when he gets back from Japan." She turned to Damon and gave him a heart-to-heart look. "Bruce is a big art lover too, you see. And with all the money he and Lila have inherited, they'll probably have a collection of their own one day. They could really use your advice!"

Jessica watched with satisfaction as Damon's face collapsed. He turned to Lila slowly, his eyes filled with cautious fear. "Bruce? Who's Bruce, Lila?"

"He's an old boyfriend, Damon," Lila said instantly, giving Jessica a quick, withering glance. "I would have told you, but it just never came up. It's not important."

"Right," Jessica said dryly.

To Jessica's irritation, however, Damon seemed to instantly accept Lila's explanation. Slipping one arm around her shoulders, he drew her to his side and faced Jessica. "Lila, this Jessica Wakefield claims to be your best friend?"

The temperature of Lila's gaze had dropped below zero. "I *try* to be patient with her. But sometimes it's awfully hard, Damon. She has troubles of her own that make her want to hurt the people closest to her."

Jessica was seething. She stood up from her seat. "Lila," she warned.

"Are you planning to leave, Ms. Wakefield?" Damon said suddenly, whipping out a computer printout from behind his lectern and scanning it. "Professor Heckman keeps an informal record of student attendance, as you may know, to keep track of their general effort in the class."

Jessica felt her stomach lurch.

"From what I can see," Damon went on, sliding his pencil across the page, "you failed to show up for last week's lecture, as well as the two previous weeks'." He looked up sternly. "Didn't you just tell me that you loved this class?"

Jessica cringed.

"For your information, Ms. Wakefield, Professor Heckman expects perfect attendance from his students, barring family or medical emergencies."

Jessica kept her hot stare firmly on Damon, but she could hear Lila's soft giggles in the background.

"Please have a seat," he demanded, his riveting green eyes fixed on Jessica's.

"No, thank you, Mr. Price," Jessica said hotly, burning with humiliation as she turned to leave. "I think I just lost my appetite for the fine arts."

Lila would pay for this. She would *pay*.

*   *   *

84

Lila's head was spinning. She was still too shocked at what Jessica had done to even speak. But before she could stew much longer, Damon was reaching for her hand.

"Friends like that I could do without," Damon said quietly.

Lila looked into his face and smiled. "I'm sorry."

Damon returned her smile, but it soon turned serious. "How old a boyfriend *is* this Bruce?"

Tears sprang to Lila's eyes. "I'm not with him, Damon. He's studying in Japan right now, and our relationship is completely on hold."

Damon looked away and pressed his lips together, as if he were trying to believe what she was saying. He nodded. "I don't want anything to come between us. You're too important to me."

"Damon," Lila said forcefully, grabbing his arms, "nothing will. Nothing can."

For a moment they just stood there, eyes locked. Lila stood on tiptoe and kissed him on the mouth. Then she turned and quietly retreated to a seat. A few moments later the first group of Damon's students began filing into the lecture hall.

"The surrealist painters were inspired by the theory that the artist could directly transpose a dream from the unconscious to the canvas without any interference from the conscious mind."

To Lila it seemed as if the whole lecture hall

was as fixated on Damon as she was. The room was silent except for the quiet scrape of note taking and Damon's intense, animated voice. As she looked around she saw that many students were on the edges of their seats, watching Damon prowl back and forth in front of the class like a panther.

She bit her lip and stared at him proudly. He was wearing a pair of khakis, a deep blue shirt, and an emerald-blue patterned tie that made his eyes appear even more green than they'd been on Friday.

"Would someone seated near the door dim the lights, please?" Damon asked.

Lila watched Damon, transfixed, as the lights fell and he switched on his slide projector. He'd seemed aware of her presence up until now, but he didn't look at her until the room was nearly dark. Then he flashed her a smile that seemed to sink directly into her heart.

Lila gulped. She knew she was falling hard for Damon. Yet lurking in the back of her mind were doubts she couldn't completely explain away.

She couldn't shake the fact that Damon hadn't given her his phone number when he clearly had a phone. And why had he taken so long to call her after their date? Had he really been too afraid of her reaction? Why did she keep getting the feeling that she knew absolutely nothing about him and that she must protect herself?

Lila drew in a sharp breath and set her lips. She didn't like this sensation of being completely out of control. But what could she do? The only thing she had to go on right now was her feelings, and her feelings told her to believe in him. *Who wouldn't?* she thought, watching him with longing as he slid onto a stool next to the slide projector.

"Salvador Dalí," Damon announced forcefully, clicking on a slide of a strange painting. "One of the most inventive of the surrealists, he painted *Return of Ulysses* in 1936 using an inkblot method to create this strange and dreamlike landscape."

Lila bit her lower lip. The painting *did* have a weird, dreamy quality to it. She blinked and looked at it again. The eerie shapes on the canvas seemed to take on different meanings the more she looked at them.

"Let's take a look at some of Dalí's contemporaries," Damon went on, clicking up a series of pictures from undulating, circular shapes, to cloudy landscapes, to detailed fantasy ink drawings.

"It was an explosive time," Damon lectured. "An inventive time in twentieth-century art. The world was changing, and artists were no longer content to mimic the old masters and impressionists. There was a fascination with the mind and this strange new concept called the unconscious that Sigmund Freud theorized about in his writings."

Lila was stirred. She barely even breathed, watching Damon speak. But as he continued, his slide projector clicked to a painting that seemed strangely familiar. She stared. It was an unusually stark oil of a blue ocean that curved away into a violet-colored sky. Where had she seen it before? The National Gallery? The Louvre? Florence? London?

"As you can see in this beautiful painting," Damon lectured, "the artist has used pattern and texture to build an angel image within the framework of the picture—thus fooling and surprising the eye as such an image would if experienced in a dream."

A dream? Lila thought. She felt her heartbeat quicken. *A dream.*

She blinked and looked at the painting again. The dream. The staircase. The painting! The painting from her dream! Right in front of her!

She drew her hands up to her face in shock. Had she actually seen the painting before? Had her unconscious mind recalled the painting in such detail that her dream revealed it to her once again? Or was it possible that she had never seen it before in her life except in her dream?

Lila trembled. There it was, as clear as it had been in her dream: the intensely blue ocean, the violet sky—and the beautiful angel emerging into view. Lila felt herself swept back into her dream. She could almost feel the silky swish of the wedding dress against her legs. She could almost smell the roses in her bouquet and see the long sweep of staircase in front of her.

Lila let her arms sag down at her sides as Damon continued his lively monologue and his surrealist slide collection flashed like a beacon on the screen.

Her heart was beating wildly in her rib cage. She'd never seen this painting in her waking life. She was sure of it. She'd only seen it in her dream. But that was impossible! Was she going completely crazy?

"Will you be testing us on the surrealists next week, Mr. Price?" a girl in the third row asked when the lights went back on.

"Only if you want me to," Damon joked.

The class groaned.

Damon stuffed his hands into the pockets of his khakis and shook his head. "No tests."

Everyone whooped.

"Look," Damon explained. "I know that Professor Heckman has hit you with plenty of tests and pop quizzes this semester. But I'd be more interested in seeing some well-researched term papers on an artist of your choice in this period. It's pretty fascinating stuff, folks. Think about it."

Damon lifted his hand to dismiss the class, then searched the crowd for Lila, who was moving slowly toward the door. At the top of the aisle she threw a subtle glance back at him, and he nodded.

He shook his head as he gathered his things and stuffed them in his briefcase. It seemed strange to have to meet Lila outside the classroom, but he knew how people could talk and how student-faculty dating was frowned on.

"See you next Wednesday," Damon called out to the retreating students. Then a moment later he left the chalky lecture room, hurried down the hallway, and burst out into the quad, where he spotted Lila sitting by herself on a bench. He shivered. The morning fog that had rolled in from the ocean still hadn't burned off. Lila's figure on the bench looked pale—almost ghostly—as he approached.

Damon caught up to her. "Hi," he said, brushing her shoulder lightly with his. But when he saw the stricken look on her face, he pulled back and looked at her carefully. "Are you OK?"

Lila was staring straight ahead. "That painting," she whispered.

"Which painting?"

"The beautiful picture of the ocean with the angel," she said in a faraway voice.

Damon nodded. *"Ocean Dream."*

Lila turned slowly to look at him. "Dream?"

He shrugged. "Yes. *Ocean Dream.* That's what the painting is called. It's not too well known, but it was somewhat famous in its time."

Lila looked away, her eyes wide with—*what?* Damon wondered. Fear? Wonder? What was going on in her head?

"It's the strangest thing, Damon," Lila said softly. "I'm sure I've seen that painting before."

90

Damon paused to think. "Well, you must have seen it during your travels. Must have been a pretty exclusive showing, though, because that piece has been in a private collection for over half a century."

"No. You don't understand." She sighed and shook her head nervously. "You're never going to believe this, Damon."

Damon narrowed his eyes. "Try me."

"OK." There was a catch in her voice. "I saw the painting in a dream."

"What?"

Lila's brown eyes searched his, as if she were begging him to believe her. "A very vivid dream. And you were in it."

Damon just stared.

Lila's fists were clenched in her lap. "I saw the painting very, very clearly."

Damon cleared his throat uncomfortably. "Lila. Come on. You've seen a lot of art in your life. It sounds like you've been to every major art museum in the Western world, not to mention all the private art showings you've been to."

Lila turned to him. The fog had begun to bead up in her hair, and her brown eyes had taken on a strange, faraway intensity. "I've *never* seen that painting."

"Except in your dream," Damon prompted her.

Lila's eyes misted. "You don't believe me."

Damon leaned back on the bench. "I just find it pretty hard to believe." He rubbed his eyes. "I mean,

I don't see how you could *dream* a painting like that."

"You said yourself that the painting had been in a private collection for a very long time," Lila said.

"Yes," Damon agreed. "I just stumbled on it last year when I was doing research in New York. Its owners let me shoot a picture of it for my lectures."

"Well, I've never seen it in a collection—a gallery—or anywhere but my dream," Lila insisted.

Damon gave Lila a serious look. Her face had paled, and he suddenly felt a wave of sympathy and love. "Are you serious?"

"More serious than I've ever been about anything," Lila told him. "It's got me a little scared, actually."

Damon took her hand. "Come on."

"What?" Lila's lovely brown eyes were wide with surprise.

"There's something I want to show you."

Damon led her away from the bench and back into the building, where they raced up the stairs to his office. He fumbled with his keys and opened the door, guiding Lila forward.

"Look," he told her, turning her toward the cloud picture hanging next to his desk. "This picture right here was painted by the same artist who painted *Ocean View*. The same artist, Lila."

Lila stared. "It's amazing."

"Do you see?" Damon asked hoarsely, taking her shoulders from behind and pressing his cheek to the side of her head. "Do you see the face in the clouds? The woman's face?"

He felt Lila's shoulders slump beneath his hands. "Oh no," she whispered.

Damon felt her knees buckle, and he slipped his arms around her to hold her steady. "Look at her closely. Look at her."

"She—she looks something like—me," she said, her voice beginning to tremble. "This is so strange. So odd. So unbelievable."

Damon whirled her around and looked into her eyes. "I've seen you before too. Right here in this painting. This painting I haven't been able to stop staring at for months."

Lila's face was white with fright. "I'm scared, Damon. I'm so scared."

"But why?" Damon answered, sliding his hands up and down her arms to reassure her. "It's fate. It's destiny. Don't you see? It's something that most people never experience."

Lila was shaking her head. Tears streamed down her face. "I don't understand."

"But it's all so clear now," Damon went on in a rush. "First I see your face in the picture that means the most to me in the world. And then you dream of a painting by the same artist. Don't you see? You're the woman in the picture. The woman I've been dreaming about. Looking for."

Lila lifted her face, and as he lowered his lips he

saw something in her expression. Confusion, fear, understanding—maybe a combination of all three.

"And now I've found her," he whispered.

Lila finally broke away, reeling from Damon's kiss. Outside his office door she could hear the usual sounds of hallway footsteps, stray conversation, laughter. But inside with Damon they had their own world.

"Damon," Lila breathed, wrapping her arms around his waist. She pressed her cheek to his shirtfront. "There's so much I don't understand."

"You're telling me," Damon said, his voice low. He rested his chin at the top of her head and hugged her tighter.

Lila returned his embrace, closing her eyes. She breathed in, sighed, then opened them again. With her head turned into Damon's chest, she could look right at the cloud picture. "It's beautiful," she whispered.

"Yeah, he was a wonderful artist," Damon said, "and an interesting guy too. He painted back in the 1930s and was pretty successful at the time, I guess."

"Mmmm," Lila murmured, breaking away gently so that she could look closely at the painting. She leaned forward and squinted. At the bottom right-hand corner she could see that the painting was signed.

At first she could make out only the last name,

painted in the artist's blurry scrawl. "Grey," Lila murmured, narrowing her eyebrows as she tried to decipher the first name.

T-h-e-o . . . Lila began making out the spelling.

"Look at the colors in this piece," Damon was whispering as he moved his hand up her back, sending shivers down to her toes.

. . . *d-o-r-e.*

Lila stepped back from the painting in horror. Slowly she drew her hands up to her mouth and gasped.

Damon's hand stopped. "What is it?" he asked.

Lila's heart was beating wildly in her chest. She opened her mouth to speak but could manage only a high, panicky breath.

Damon turned Lila around, and she could see that his green eyes were filled with concern. "What's wrong?"

"Theodore," Lila whispered in a hoarse voice.

"Yes," Damon answered. "Theodore Grey. The painter. That was his name."

Lila felt her knees buckle, and Damon caught her forearms just before she began to fall.

Theodore, Lila thought wildly. The man she adored in her dream. The man she married, whose ocean picture hung in his home. His name had been Theodore too.

Damon lifted her chin and looked at her closely. "What's wrong? What's happening?"

Lila pressed her lips together and shook her head.

He already thinks I'm crazy, she thought. *If I tell him about the Theodore in my dream, he'll think I'm completely insane. Or could he just be trying to make me feel that way?*

"Nothing's wrong," Lila said instead, forcing herself to quiet her shaking body.

I can't tell him any more about the dream right now, she resolved as he bent down to kiss her gently on the lips. *I could lose him if I do. And I'm not ready to do that even if I'm not completely sure about him. The truth will have to wait.*

Chapter Seven

"I am going to *kill* him!" Jessica screamed as she stormed into her dorm room and flung her books on the bed. She crossed her arms hard against her chest and paced back and forth.

How could he humiliate me like that? she thought angrily. She grabbed her hair as if she could yank away the pain of the appalling scene in the lecture hall. *Lila's new boyfriend is supposed to be a professional, not a bully. Where does he come off threatening me with a lousy grade?*

Jessica's teeth clenched even more tightly as her thoughts turned to Lila. The whole horrible scene flashed before her eyes once again: Lila just standing there, smirking as Damon Price ridiculed her.

What a complete traitor! Jessica thought, remembering the hours and hours she had stood at *Lila's* side during times of trouble. Jessica remembered all the times she'd given Lila advice about clothes and guys and consoled her through her various romantic breakups, minor weight gains, and exam crises. Not to mention the way she came to Lila's rescue after Tisiano died!

Come to think of it—where would Lila be without me? Jessica thought, staring at her reflection in the mirror. She'd actually set her alarm for 7 A.M. that morning so that she would have plenty of time to get ready for her lecture.

Just thinking about how carefully she had washed and curled her hair for the event made her blood boil in her veins. She stared angrily at the way she'd curled and then double curled her silky hair until it was an extra-thick cloud of blond fluffed strategically about her pretty face.

She grabbed her hairbrush and snarled at the lovely picture she made in the mirror. If Lila hadn't been there, hogging the cute new TA, Jessica was convinced he would have fallen for her instead.

Before she could stop herself, Jessica flipped her hair upside down and began furiously brushing out her curls.

I am going to kill that Damon Price, she vowed. *And then I'm going to kill Lila.*

Jessica flipped her head back up as tears began to fill her blue-green eyes. Her hair stuck out like a crazy, strawlike mass. Ruined.

She threw herself down on the bed, grabbed

the university directory, and ran a glossy nail down the list of important-sounding offices.

"Mmmm. Dean of students. Office of the president. Vice president for academic affairs," Jessica muttered as she snatched up the cordless phone. "I'm sure some of these folks would like to know that one of their precious new TAs is pursuing a *totally* inappropriate romantic relationship with a young female student."

But Jessica paused, her hand over the dial. Who was she *really* angry with? Damon Price—a guy she didn't even know? Or Lila Fowler—her closest friend, who had just completely betrayed her?

"Lila," Jessica drawled, setting down the phone. "Lila's the one who always gets exactly what she wants, no matter who she steps on in the process. And who else has she betrayed besides little old me?"

Bruce Patman, that's who.

Jessica slid her glance across the room until it came to a halt at her desk, littered with shampoo bottles, popcorn kernels, soda cans, and dusty, unopened textbooks. Sticking out of the mess was an airmail envelope. Her lips formed into a small, sly smile. There was only one thing she could do. Only one thing she really wanted to do.

"So you're counting the days until you see Lila again, huh, Bruce?" Jessica whispered to herself. "Well, I have some information that might make you change your mind."

Sighing with satisfaction, she picked up the phone again and dialed the operator. "I'd like information for Japan," Jessica said in a clear voice, suddenly happy and focused for the first time all morning. "As in the *country* of Japan?"

"We'll have to connect you to our international long-distance directory operator, ma'am."

Jessica made a face. "Well, could you do that, please?"

"May I have the number you're calling from?"

Jessica gave out the number, gritting her teeth.

"Directory assistance for Japan," another operator said in a brisk voice.

Jessica took a deep breath. "Yes, I'm trying to get the number of a student at the University of Kyoto. . . ."

Static roared over the telephone line, and Jessica thought she heard someone rattling on in the background in Japanese.

"Kyoto!" Jessica yelled.

There was another wave of static. "Kyoto-Fu?" a distant voice called out.

"University of Kyoto," Jessica shouted. "Student!"

"OK, OK," she heard the faint voice again.

"English! I'm calling from America!" Jessica wailed.

"May I help you?" Another voice came onto the line.

"Patman!" Jessica spat. "Bruce Patman. He's a

student at the University of Kyoto, and I need his number."

"You'll have to call a different directory assistance operator, ma'am. Let me give you that number. Please hold."

"What?"

"*Hold*, please."

"Forget it!" Jessica shouted, grabbing the letter out of the envelope and quickly scanning it.

I am counting the days until I see you again. Love, Bruce.

"Someone's got to tell him," Jessica muttered, searching for a piece of paper and an envelope. She found a pencil and began scrawling quickly across a sheet of plain computer paper.

Dear Bruce,

It breaks my heart to tell you this, but you need to know that Lila has not been the faithful girl she promised to be when you left. She's cheating on you, Bruce. And it's not just anyone. It's an older guy. Her art history TA, actually. A guy named Damon Price. Someone had to tell you, and I guess it had to be me.

Jessica signed the letter with a flourish, carefully copied the return address on the envelope, then rummaged through Elizabeth's desk drawer until she found five airmail stamps. She stuck them all on the envelope and dashed out her dorm-room door, headed for the nearest mailbox.

A valuable letter, Jessica thought. *Valuable information for Bruce. And a valuable lesson for Lila: Don't mess with Jessica Wakefield.*

The masked ball had only just begun as Flora came sailing down the broad staircase, flooded with light and strung with hundreds of black and white balloons. Below her in the vast reception room was a throng of brightly dressed guests, dancing gaily to the music of the large orchestra Theodore had hired for the occasion.

Flora paused and looked down at her own dress, a billowing, off-the-shoulder Louis XIV era gown with a plunging neckline and dramatically pinched-in waist. She held an elaborate fan in one hand and in the other a small wand with a tiny mask at its end.

She and Theodore had spent weeks planning this party, and she could already tell it was a smashing success. The party would show everyone how happy they were together—and how they wanted to share their joy with the world.

Flora sank happily into the crush of humming, chattering, laughing guests, each one dressed more outrageously than the next. Before she could take a breath, a man in tights and Elizabethan dress handed her a glass of bubbling champagne, followed by a woman in a slinky Cleopatra gown who poured more into her glass. Flora threw back her head with laughter as she threaded her way through the crowd. There were princesses, vampires, Charlie Chaplins, dozens of silver-screen-ready blond bombshells, and even a couple elaborately dressed as two halves of a painting.

Flora moved forward, chatting and mingling under the room's glittering chandelier, checking the champagne supply, sending back empty hors d'oeuvre trays, scolding slow-moving serving girls, and kissing as many of her celebrated guests as possible.

"Everyone who's anyone in the Hamptons is here, darling!" the woman dressed in the Cleopatra dress called out to Flora. "Marvelous!"

"Your husband's such a genius, my dear," a middle-aged woman murmured in Flora's ear. "We bought one of his ocean pieces three years ago, and we *treasure* it."

"I'm so glad," she said absently, inching forward on tiptoe, searching for a glimpse of Theodore.

Finally she saw him come in from wherever he'd been hiding. He was approaching her now, smiling and shaking hands as he threaded his way through the bobbing crowd. Flora sighed. Theodore always looked so wonderful in black tie. But he looked a little tired right now. Since their wedding four months ago he'd spent long hours painting in his studio. He even looked a little different now. His hair was longer, almost wild, and he'd grown a goatee that gave his face a harsher, more mysterious angle.

I'll have to talk to him about that, she reminded herself.

Flora sighed again. She hadn't admitted it to anyone, but lately she'd seen more of the servants than she had of Theodore. Still, he was a busy man. He was an artist in demand, at the peak of his artistic powers. And for right now at least Flora felt uplifted by the giddiness of the crowd. The music and lights were spinning around her like an intoxicating cloud, making her forget her few silly cares. At this wonderful moment all Flora wanted was to feel the happiness and abandon that only a huge, lavish party could provide.

A hand slid around her waist, and she suddenly found herself dancing. Not in the arms of her husband yet but instead with a terribly good-looking man in a pirate's costume. Flora tossed her head and gave her body completely to the strong arm that held her. She felt a thrill. There was the spicy smell of his shaving cream, the feeling of masculine control leading her around the dance floor to the rhythm of the music. She closed her eyes, imagining that her unknown partner was really Theodore. A moment later she opened them and realized that she had taken center stage and everyone in the ballroom was watching her and cheering her on.

There was a pause in the dance, and Flora felt a tap at her shoulder.

"May I have this dance, please, Mrs. Grey?"

She turned and smiled happily at Theodore, who stood at attention, trying to control his eager smile while the entire gathering watched. He pulled her away from her pirate and spun her around until she felt faint with joy and dizziness.

"Having a good time, my love?" Theodore murmured in her ear.

Flora felt his warmth spreading all over her body, and when he dropped down to brush a kiss on her lips, she almost didn't have the strength to keep on dancing. "The party's wonderful . . . and you're adorable," Flora replied.

Theodore spun her around again, but this time she kept her gaze fixed on his mesmerizing green eyes. In the background she could hear the patter of applause.

"Here, here!" she heard someone say.

"Isn't love grand?"

"Still newlyweds, aren't they?"

When the music ended and Theodore finished spinning her, she drew her hands up to her face in laughter.

Theodore bowed to the applause of the crowd and then to Flora. "Thank you, darling," he said. "I'm going to fetch you a cold drink." He stood very still and gave her an alluring look. "Don't run away."

Flora laughed. "I won't, my dear." She turned

and threaded her way through the crush as the band struck up another dance number. Then at the corner of the dance floor she sat down by herself.

"Mrs. Grey?"

Flora turned toward the young woman who'd just sat down next to her. Her red lips glistened in her powdered face, and her eyes seemed to gleam with curiosity. Unlike the rest of her wildly costumed guests, this woman was wearing a simple navy blue suit and hat. A matching handbag hung on her arm.

"Yes?" Flora replied.

The woman inched closer and gave her a confidential look before sticking out her hand. "Margaret Hancock. I'm with *The Examiner.*"

Flora shook her hand cautiously. "I see. What do you do for *The Examiner*, Miss Hancock?"

The woman stared at her with what looked to Flora like disbelief before putting her head close to Flora's. "I'm *Margaret Hancock.* Is it possible that you don't read my society column? That's why I'm here. Biggest night of the season and all."

Flora shifted uncomfortably. She detested the gossip columns. They relied on rumor, half-truths, and sensationalism to sell newspapers. What's more, Flora knew they traded on the privacy and sanity of people like her. Still, she smiled politely. "I'm so glad you could come, Miss Hancock." She gestured toward the party. "Please enjoy yourself."

"Mrs. Grey," the woman said quickly, standing

up too. "May I have a few minutes with you?"

Flora stared back at the woman's serious expression. "What do you want, Miss Hancock?"

Miss Hancock cocked her head and smiled out of the corner of her mouth. "*The Examiner* is always interested in writing about the East Coast's most interesting couple. You wouldn't want us to rely on rumor and innuendo and not consult you at all, would you?"

Flora narrowed her eyes. "What rumor?"

Miss Hancock motioned at the door to the terrace outside the ballroom. "Please."

Flora paused. There was no reason in the world why she should tear herself away from the most important party of her life to grant an interview to a society-page reporter. But the woman had such a mysterious, all-knowing look. Flora found herself compelled to lead her out one of the ballroom's side doors onto the empty terrace.

She sat down slowly. Through the tall terrace windows she could see the jam-packed party bouncing in full swing, like a distant carnival. Out here the rose vines along the terrace railing rustled in the faint evening breeze. The reporter waited for a young strolling couple to descend into the garden out of earshot.

"Thank you, Mrs. Grey," she said finally.

"You're a determined woman," Flora said.

Miss Hancock eyed her. Then she crossed her legs and inched toward Flora. "I'll come right to

107

the point, Mrs. Grey. I'm going to write a column for tomorrow's morning edition saying that you and your husband threw the most brilliant, lavish party of the season."

Flora felt a thrill. She'd worked hard on this party, mostly to please Theo. But a positive write-up in the paper would be nice too. Still . . .

"Well, thank you, Miss Hancock. That will be lovely. We've worked very hard to please our friends tonight."

Miss Hancock narrowed her eyes. "No problem at all. But you must answer an important question."

"And what is that?" Flora asked with a polite smile.

"Is there any truth to all these stories about how your husband's family fortune is slipping away?" the reporter asked bluntly, her pencil now poised over her notebook.

Flora's lips parted in shock. "My husband is a wealthy man. I've never had any reason to doubt it."

The woman raised her eyebrows. "Really?"

Flora started to stand up. "Actually I'm *quite* offended by your tactless question, Miss Hancock," she huffed.

The woman looked up sharply at Flora. "I'm sorry, Mrs. Grey. But you're a profoundly famous and public couple in this part of the world. People notice things. People ask questions. And people talk."

Flora drew herself up. Had she been living in a dream world? It was true that she and Theo were well-known, but it wasn't Flora's nature to dwell on what people thought of them. She always felt as if she and Theo lived alone in their own private world—on display only when they chose, such as on nights like this. Tonight, however, Flora realized that she'd been a fool.

"And what are people talking about, Miss Hancock?" Flora finally asked in a chilly voice.

"People are saying that Theodore Grey has lost his magic touch," she shot back. "That he hasn't sold a painting in two years."

"What?" Flora cried, taking a step back. "That's untrue!"

The woman seemed unaffected by Flora's distress. In fact, she was actually watching her with a kind of cool amusement. "There's another story making its rounds in society circles as well. People are also saying that your marriage to Theodore Grey is on the rocks."

"That's a lie!" Flora said, unable to keep from raising her voice.

"Then I'll report it as such," Miss Hancock said, lifting her chin.

Flora was trembling. "Why are people saying these things? We've only been married four months. We're very much in love, and my husband's painting is going very well. He's in his studio constantly. . . ."

Flora could hear a door to the ballroom open

behind her. Miss Hancock gave a quick glance, stood up, nodded to Flora, and walked away down a short flight of steps into the dark garden.

Flora watched in horror as she disappeared, and after only a few moments she felt a hand on her shoulder. She jumped.

"Flora?"

"Theodore!" Flora cried out, turning.

She felt his grip tightening on her arm as she started to stand up, and when she turned around, she gasped. His face was pinched into a tight, angry mass.

"What's wrong, darling?" Flora asked.

Theodore gripped her upper arm even tighter. The look in his green eyes was cold and lifeless. "Would you come with me for a moment, dear?"

Flora let out a soft cry as her husband began to pull her firmly down the darkened terrace. She tried in vain to keep up with him as he rounded the corner and headed toward the library door, but she very nearly tripped on her ball gown. "Why are you holding me so tightly, Theodore? Stop it!"

Theodore roughly opened the library door and motioned for her to enter.

"Theodore!" Flora cried out as she hurried into the dark room, rubbing her arm. "What's this all about?"

"Who were you talking to just now?" Theodore asked, his voice tight.

Flora flinched. Her husband had never spoken

to her like that. She turned, her eyes traveling up his stiff white shirtfront, to the perfect black tie, to his reddening, furious face. Slowly she sat down on one of the library's huge leather sofas and stared at the squares of moonlight filtering through the tall windows. The noise of the party was a distant, throbbing beat, and the books on the wall seemed to stare down at her in judgment.

"Well?" Theodore said in a loud voice.

Flora turned. Theodore was standing motionless in the moonlight, his arms crossed over his broad chest, his mouth a tight line.

"That was Margaret Hancock," Flora said, trying not to let her voice shake. "She's a reporter—"

"A reporter with *The Examiner,*" Theodore interrupted. "A *society* reporter," he repeated, his voice rising slightly. "So you *were* aware of who you were speaking to."

"Yes," Flora replied. "She introduced herself, and—"

"You decided to actually *respond* to her silly questions."

"Well, I had no idea what she was going to ask me," Flora answered. "Do you know this woman? Do you know what she was asking?"

Theodore let out a despairing laugh. "Of *course* I know who she is. She's been hounding me for weeks."

"Well, how did she get in?"

Theodore lowered his angry face right down

to hers. "Someone—must have—given—her—an invitation, dear."

Flora drew back. "I had no idea she would—"

"You," Theodore began with an abrupt shout, raising a finger into the air, "have *no* business speaking with others about our personal life!"

Flora gasped in shock. "Darling—"

"You have no right!" He paced toward the bookshelf, his hands clasped tightly behind his back.

Flora started to get up. "But Theo," she said in a shaky voice. "She's just spreading rumors. What difference does it make when these stories are untrue to begin with?"

Theodore spun around, his eyes blazing. He cupped his hands around his mouth and shouted, *"Because the stories* are *true!"*

Flora stumbled toward him, tears flooding her eyes. "What are you talking about?"

"I'm saying," he said, his voice dropping to a growling whisper, "that Miss Hancock's version of the truth is correct."

"About the money? Or about—"

"Yes, about the money!" Theodore raged. "My inheritance! I've wasted it. I've squandered it. I—I thought I could make up for it—with my paintings, but . . ." He trailed off, his arms limp with defeat.

Flora's knees were weak. "But . . . but what about this party? How could we afford the party? And—and everything else?"

112

Theodore turned and made two fists in the air. "I borrowed it. I borrowed it from Thomas, my brother," he cried. "And he loved every minute of it. He loved watching me crawl on my knees, begging him—"

"But you said you hadn't talked to Thomas in years."

Theodore began to cry. "I hate him. But I had no choice."

Flora rushed toward her husband to embrace him. But suddenly Theodore stepped back, his eyes still filled with tears yet wild and unforgiving. He reached for a book from the shelf behind him and held it up like a weapon. "Don't come near me, Flora."

"We can work things out," Flora begged him. "You'll see."

"Not after what you've done!" Theodore shouted. "If word gets out that no one's buying my paintings, then I'm ruined. Don't you see? People pay high prices for art that is difficult to obtain." He thrust his hand into the air, pointing toward the ceiling, above which was his studio. "My art is not difficult to obtain, Flora! It's sitting up there, untouched. Dozens of canvases. Unsold!"

Flora was sobbing. She reached her arms out for him. "We can move away, darling. Start all over again."

"The party was an act, Flora!" Theodore went on crazily. "An act to show how rich and successful I am because my art is in demand. If anyone finds out it's a lie, we're ruined. We can't run away from that."

"Yes, we can!" Flora screamed.

"No!" Theodore shouted, throwing the book across the room, where it smashed against an antique tea set. "I'm finished! Ruined!" he yelled, yanking books off the shelf and throwing them crazily on the floor, against the furniture, against the priceless Tiffany lamps at the window.

"Stop!" Flora screamed. She rushed toward Theodore, her hands clasped against her ears.

But just before she reached him, Theodore in his anger had begun pulling heavy volumes out of the bookshelf. Before she realized what was happening, he'd flung one in the direction of her head.

For a split second Flora saw the sharp-cornered book spinning crazily through the air, propelled by the sudden, almost superhuman strength of her husband. Then the motion of the book seemed to stall, as if she were watching it in slow motion.

She watched the gilt-edged pages flipping dizzily through space, sending sparks of light as in an explosion. She saw its red cover like a streak of blood in the air. Then she felt the sharp point of the book's corner against her temple, sending her head smashing to the ground, where the light gradually faded from yellow to gray to a deep, dreamlike black and utter silence.

Chapter Eight

"No!" Lila called out. She sat up in bed, clawing at the air with her hands. "No!"

A long moment passed before Lila opened her eyes and heard the telephone in her apartment ringing. Thick fog pressed in at her bedroom window, and outside, the dripping branches hung still and stark in the dim morning light.

Slowly Lila lowered her head to the pillow and drew her hands up to her eyes. The nightmare again. Even worse than before. She winced as the insistent telephone rang over and over. *Probably Jessica,* she thought irritably.

"Hello?"

There was silence on the other end of the line.

"Hello?" Lila repeated, the sound of the phone somehow bringing her back to a comforting reality. She yawned. "Look, Jessica, you're acting like a kook. I know you're mad. So why don't you call me back when you're ready to talk?"

Lila hung up and stared at the ceiling, the dream still ringing vividly in her mind. The horror of Theodore's attack was fresh, but the excitement of the party was what she really wanted to remember. A part of her longed to return to the vast ballroom, draped in satin, and dance to the music of her very own orchestra, looking like a stunning version of Marie Antoinette.

And Damon looked so gorgeous in black tie, Lila thought longingly before she remembered once again that in the dream he hadn't been called Damon at all. He had been Theodore.

"Theodore Grey," Lila whispered. She bit her thumbnail and pulled her sheets up around her neck, trying to think.

Lila's thoughts drifted back to Damon, nagged by the eerie sensation that she was somehow leading two lives at the same time. *Yet the two lives are completely different,* Lila reassured herself, slipping out of bed. *And my wide-awake life is definitely the one I'd pick.*

She pulled on her French silk robe and padded toward the kitchen for coffee, contemplating Damon and Theodore. Their faces were the same, but Damon and Theodore were as different as she could imagine. Damon was gentle, loving, and vulnerable. Theodore was wild, desperate, and menacing. One face: two completely different personalities.

She frowned. Still, she didn't understand how someone as sweet and loving as Damon could have turned into such a monster in her dream. She could imagine Damon as a dashing artist but not as anyone who could hurt her the way Theodore was hurting Flora.

Lila's hand froze on her refrigerator door.

"Then again," she whispered.

The book, she thought. *Damon did hit my head with a book, even if it was an accident. He hit my head hard, just like Theo hit Flora's.*

Lila shut the refrigerator door and walked back down the hall to her bathroom, where she stared intently at her face in her large Florentine silver-framed mirror. She pushed her silky hair off her face, and the face of Flora stared back at her.

Damon isn't Theodore, she told her reflection. *Damon was terribly sweet after the accident. He rocked me gently. He took me home. He called to make sure I was OK. He couldn't be the same man as your Theodore, Flora. He just couldn't.*

Lila shivered, remembering Theodore's desperate, angry face. He'd been so determined to save his reputation, and yet it seemed as if his creativity was leading him on a path to destruction. Maybe that was why he needed to blame it on Flora. . . .

She shuddered, reached absently for a bottle of lotion, and squeezed a ribbon of it into her hand. Why was she making such a big deal about a

117

dream? Dreams were just bits and pieces of images and feelings from her waking life, weren't they? Dwelling on this dream too much might make her start thinking of Damon as Theodore—and no two people could be more different.

She glanced at the small clock on her bathroom counter. She had an hour and a half before her ten o'clock literature class began, and she felt strangely out of control, which was *not* how Lila usually felt.

She knew it was the dream, and she wanted to do something about it, but until she was halfway through picking out her outfit, she wasn't sure what.

Then it hit her. Theodore Grey. He'd obviously been an actual painter. A surrealist painter. And if he was famous enough for Damon to be lecturing about him at SVU, he was probably famous enough to be found in . . .

The library, Lila thought. She was pretty sure she knew where the library was. And even if she couldn't figure out how to look up Theodore Grey, there were always decrepit-looking reference librarians hanging around. They'd probably get a big thrill out of helping her research her mystery man.

It was ten o'clock Thursday morning, and Damon had just finished grading the last paper from his pile. With a flourish he assigned it a B-plus, then stuck his feet up on his desk and stretched. Usually his morning hours involved a crush of visitors and student appointments, but today his office was strangely, blissfully quiet. He smiled at the print on the wall.

"Well, Lila." He spoke softly to the picture. "I'm crazy about you. But I'm a little worried too. I'll admit it: I want everything between us to be perfect. Please don't have any more nightmares."

He took a swig of coffee and knelt down next to one of his bookshelves, running his finger along the volumes on the bottom shelf. "Mmmm," he muttered, "here you are, Theo."

Damon pulled out a slender volume, sat down in his overstuffed chair, and settled the book on his lap, scanning the title: *The Art of Theodore Grey: A Vision of Madness.*

Damon chuckled, opening the book to the color plates inside. He'd just begun studying Grey's paintings a few months ago, especially his later works. "You weren't mad, Theo. You just had more imagination than the rest of us."

A vivid blue-and-green painting caught his eye, and he turned the book on its side so he could admire Grey's skillful use of color and perspective. A perfectly shaped tree, in full leaf, stood against a bright blue sky. He smiled. What was interesting about Grey was the way he tricked the eye. The tree, a uniform shape at first glance, was actually a complex arrangement of leaf and branch. And a closer look revealed—as in so many of his other pictures—the intricately detailed face of a woman.

The same woman.

Lila.

Damon drew back his head as if he'd been shocked. It was uncanny how closely the woman in the Grey paintings resembled Lila Fowler. Damon kept turning the pages. There was a lush painting of the inside of a flower. A moon in a starry sky. A mountain reflected in intricate detail from a lake.

Damon felt a chill. Though the paintings were familiar to him, he'd never seen so much revealed below the surface of paint and canvas. It was true that a woman's face was hidden within each picture. And all the faces seemed to be Lila's.

He rubbed his eyes. *Am I going crazy, Theo? People say that you did. Am I working too hard, like you did? Or is your unusual, haunting art doing strange things to my mind?*

"Or is it just love?" Damon whispered. He looked up from the book in wonder, his face suddenly flushed. "Is that why I keep seeing your face, Lila?"

Damon flipped through the remaining color plates in the book until he came to the last one and felt a clutch in his heart. The painting in front of him was completely different from the rest. He'd forgotten. Instead of an ocean or plant or cloud, Theodore Grey had actually painted a person. A portrait of a woman, in fact.

The same woman whose face he'd hidden in his paintings for so many years.

"Only this time, Theodore, something has made you angry," Damon whispered.

He stared at the picture, which appeared to be a conventional portrait of a beautiful woman, seated on a gilt chair, wearing a flowing white dress. Through his brilliant use of color the woman's skin seemed to radiate light from within, and the smile on her face was a smile of love.

Damon shuddered. Instead of being content with the lovely portrait, the artist had vandalized it horribly. Crude slash marks crisscrossed the painting, and at the neck, where one particularly harsh cut was made, the artist had purposely dripped red blood from the opening.

The effect was a shocking vision of brutality. Of hatred. Of frustration.

Damon felt a rush of fear just looking at it. Without hesitating he dug into his jacket for his wallet and pulled out Lila's phone number. He dialed it quickly, but there was only her answering machine.

"*Hello. This is Lila Fowler. I'm sorry I am unable to take your call. . . .*

Damon opened his mouth to speak, to say—anything. But no words came out. He slammed down the phone, trembling and searching his heart for an explanation. What *were* his feelings?

121

Fear? Love? Disgust? He couldn't find the words to express whatever it was.

But for a split second Damon felt as if he were looking beyond his own life into another place, another time, long ago—like a bad memory he wanted to forget.

Lila hurried down the stacks of the university library, glancing down at the number the research librarian had penciled on a slip of paper for her. She shivered. Her hand-tailored wool flannel duster was damp from the persistent ocean fog that had enshrouded the campus.

"Nine-hundred-sixteen dot one-three-five," she whispered to herself, stopping at the end of a stack, then turning to the right, where a stack of volumes ran clear down to the windows on the south side of the library.

Lila sighed. *There must be a quarter mile of books in this stack alone. Why do they have to make it so difficult for people to find one?*

Creeping down the narrow aisle, Lila finally found the 916 volumes. She ran a finger along the spines of the passing books, narrowing the numbers down until she realized that the book she wanted was at the very bottom of the stack.

Lila knelt down. Her pale peach Italian silk pants swept against the column of dusty books, leaving a wedge of dark grime.

"Drat," Lila hissed, digging into her leather bag for a hankie, but she suddenly lost her balance and landed on her bottom. She sighed with exasperation. "At least I have a good view of the titles now."

Lila set down her bag and crossed her legs. Then she leaned forward and scanned the last few titles on the shelf until she matched the number and pulled out a slim, weathered volume. The next moment a wave of dust reached her nose and she sneezed violently.

Lila stood up, brushed the dirt off her coat and pants, then sneezed another two times.

"Excuse me."

"What?" Lila turned just as a large guy carrying a grubby wet backpack squeezed past her. She gritted her teeth as the backpack dragged along the delicate fabric of her coat.

"This better be a *very* good book," Lila muttered under her breath as she headed for a nearby table, accidentally stepping on a large wad of gum on the way. She turned her ankle to see the glob on the sole of her brand-new pale peach calf-suede shoes.

Then she opened the book and stared at the title page. *"Theodore Grey: A Brief Life of the Surrealist,"* Lila read as she walked slowly to the table. "By Cameron Phillips, Hagar and Sons, Publishers, 1947."

Lila drew her hands away from the book. She nervously dug back into her pocket for her hankie and felt her heart begin to pound as she twisted it between her fingers.

What am I looking for? she wondered silently. *Bits and pieces of his life? Something that will explain away my dreams or soothe my crazed nerves?*

Lila bit her lip. Maybe she was looking for a reminder of some kind. Maybe she *had* seen a Theodore Grey painting before and had somehow absorbed his name and his face along with the image of the painting. Maybe something in the book would jog her memory.

Slowly Lila picked up the book again and gently turned the first pages of mildewed text. Her heart speeded up as she saw that a black-and-white photo was opposite the title page, though covered with a protective film of tissue.

With a trembling hand she slipped her finger up to the top corner and slowly turned the tissue away from the photograph.

"Oh no," Lila gasped, her eyes widening in shock.

She stared at the face. She took in the classically handsome features. The clear, quizzical eyes. The high, serious brow and subtle smile. An eerie feeling flooded through her, as if she were staring into the eyes of a ghost. It was all there.

It was Damon's face. Yet underneath the photograph was a different name: Theodore Grey.

Lila felt the floor swoon under her and steadied her hands by placing them in front of her on the library table. She closed her eyes, trying desperately to wrap her mind around the strange events of the past few days. But nothing made sense.

Her hands were shaking violently now, but she continued to turn the pages as if something were waiting for her—a clue, a small piece of comfort or sanity. . . .

"Oh no," Lila cried out again, this time letting the book fall out of her hands and crash to the floor.

She closed her eyes, the words on the page still burning into her mind.

Chapter Two
"Flora and Theodore Grey: A Marriage Doomed by Passion"

"Flora," she whispered. "Theodore's wife. Her name was Flora."

Damon had returned his Theodore Grey book to the shelf and was pacing in front of his tiny office window, trying to make sense of what he'd seen in the eerie paintings.

Still, he reminded himself, he had an eleven o'clock lecture, and it was only forty minutes away. There were notes to prepare and several small items to research. He turned and faced his desk with determination. Grey's paintings had affected him in a strange way. But then, he'd always been fascinated and a little spooked by the artist. It wasn't anything new.

He'd been making notes, however, for only a few minutes when he heard an urgent knocking at his door.

Damon frowned and jumped up. When he opened his office door, his eyes opened wide. It was Lila, but it wasn't the Lila he knew. Her face, pinched and pale, had a wild look to it as if she'd just seen a ghost. As usual she wore a beautiful outfit, but the collar of her coat had been yanked up on one side and her chestnut hair hung in limp clumps.

"Wh-What happened?" he stammered. "Are you hurt?"

For a moment Lila just stood in the middle of his office, a distant look on her ragged face, as if she were trying to collect her thoughts. Then she slowly drew up one hand and covered her mouth with it, sobbing.

Damon rubbed the back of his neck. "Lila? What . . ."

Lila quickly turned to face him, stepped forward, and wrapped her arms tightly around his waist. She pressed her cheek into his shirtfront and let out a few frantic, muffled sobs. "I'm sorry. I shouldn't have come. I just got so—so scared."

Damon pulled back, holding her shoulders. "Scared of what, Lila?"

"Your face . . . her . . . name . . . ," Lila stammered. Damon could feel her arms trembling and led her to his big chair, where he knelt down beside her and took her hand.

"What face? Whose name?"

Lila sobbed once more, then steadied herself, pushing her fingers into her forehead and sniffing. "His name too." She looked up at him, her face wet with tears. "It's the dreams I've been having, Damon. I haven't told you everything."

Damon frowned. "You told me you'd dreamed Theodore Grey's ocean painting before I showed the slide in class. And you said that I was in the dream too."

"And do you believe me?" Lila asked, her expression earnest.

Damon reached up and stroked the side of her face. "Of course I do. Stranger things have happened."

Lila's eyes opened wider, and she began to nod. "Yes. I know. Stranger things *have* happened."

Damon stared at Lila's pale, distraught face. Black mascara was melting down her wet cheeks, and her lips had begun to shiver with agitation. What had suddenly happened to this composed and beautiful woman he'd met only a few days ago? Did he really know her as well as he'd thought?

Lila gripped his hand. "I saw the painting in my dream, but I also saw us in the dream. You were the artist who painted that picture, and your name was Theodore—even before I knew who he was." She took a long, shaky breath. "And in my dream I was Theodore's wife, and I was called Flora."

"What?"

Lila nodded. "That was his wife's name, Damon. I looked it up just now in the library."

Damon narrowed his eyes and reached for his Theodore Grey volume. "That's impossible."

"But it happened," Lila cried. "I'm scared, Damon. Scared."

Damon flipped through his book until he found a mention of Theodore Grey's wife, Flora, a frequent model for his paintings. His eyes darted back up to Lila's tear-stained face. "You're right, Lila. Her name was Flora. I didn't know that."

Lila bolted from the chair and began frantically pacing the tiny office. "It was all so real, Damon," she said in a rush. "We were in a huge house. Your house. In the first dream it was our wedding day, and there were people everywhere. Everyone was dressed the way they did in the 1930s. That's where I saw the picture of the ocean, with the angel."

Damon stared. He was seriously worried about Lila now. She just wasn't making any sense. "That's impossible."

"It's true!" Lila cried.

"Get ahold of yourself!" Damon begged her. "You're not well. You need sleep."

Lila covered her face with her hands and shook her head. "It was the second dream that terrified me, Damon. We were throwing a masked ball . . .

128

and a reporter wanted to know if it was true we'd lost all our money. You were furious."

"Me?" Damon said in confusion. "That wasn't me. It was someone in your dream."

Lila's face twisted in agony. "But it *was* you, Damon. Theodore Grey looked just like you. And his voice—"

"Lila!"

Lila wasn't listening. Her eyes didn't see him but were focused instead on something misty and far away. "You grabbed me and dragged me to our library. You said we were ruined unless you could convince the art world that your paintings were selling. It was awful, Damon, the way you—"

Damon grabbed her arms and crushed them in his hands. The sound of her voice pulled the anger up from someplace deep inside him. *"It wasn't me!"*

Lila sobbed, turning her face away from him. "You grabbed me just like you're doing now. You took a book from the shelf . . . and threw it . . . smashing . . . everything. When I tried to stop you—"

"Lila!"

"You threw the book at me. It hit my head just like it did in your apartment Friday. I fell—"

"Stop it, Lila," Damon heard himself say, his voice suddenly cold and fierce. "It wasn't me."

Lila collapsed back into the chair, still crying. Tears dripped through the fingers that covered her face. "It was," she whispered. "You were my husband, and you were hurting me—"

"I've heard enough, Lila," Damon said, his voice like ice now. "I've never hurt you. We're not married. And for that matter, we met only a few days ago."

"Please—"

"You've been having some terrible dreams," Damon said, trying to calm the fury she'd aroused in him. What could she be thinking, talking like this? About marriage? About him being a brutal wife beater? Why was she doing this?

"I think you need to rest," Damon finally said.

Lila just sat there sobbing.

But Damon felt himself unable to comfort her. There was something so untamed and primal in her voice. He had to pull back. He closed his eyes and crossed his arms tightly across his chest. She was frightening him, but it was impossible to explain to her why she was—especially in her frenzied state.

"The names, the similarities of the paintings," Damon heard himself explain coolly, "they're just coincidences. It's your mind playing tricks on you. It's amazing how the mind can do that, you know. How it can torture you."

Lila stood up quickly, her face hard and white. "This is *not* my imagination. Something strange is happening to me. To us."

But Damon couldn't respond. He was worried about Lila, but he found it impossible to believe what she was telling him. What was he supposed to do? Go along with her and get her to the help she needed? Or try to talk her out of it? Slowly he walked around his desk and sat down, lowering his head to his papers.

"I came to you for help," Lila said, her voice growing dignified. "I wouldn't have come if I didn't think it was important. If I didn't think you cared."

Damon pressed his lips together and began shuffling a stack of papers in front of him, unable to speak.

"At least I *thought* you cared," Lila said softly.

Damon lifted his head and looked at her ragged, tear-stained face with an odd sense of detachment. "Lila. I have a class in twenty minutes. I have to prepare."

"Fine, Damon," Lila said, her pale face suddenly flushing pink with indignation. "You just go ahead and do that. I'm leaving. And I promise I won't be bothering you anymore."

Chapter
Nine

"Theo?"

Flora had awakened from a fitful sleep, her sheets twisted and damp around her body.

"Theo? Are you there?"

She rolled over and saw that his side of the bed was empty. Moonlight dropped through the tall bedroom window, casting a dull light on the satin covers strewn across the bed. All about the room she could see her cluttered dressing tables, piles of disheveled clothes, and books scattered about the floor.

She rose from her bed and wrapped her tattered dressing gown about her body as she moved toward the window. Spread out before her was the once formal garden, now a landscape of weeds, ragged hedges, and withered flower beds.

Sighing, she turned and wandered out into the long hallway connecting her room with Theodore's studio. The walls, now empty of pictures and rugs, made her footsteps echo hollow and sad. Each bare space she passed reminded her of another precious heirloom taken away as the others had been, one by one.

Everything gone. The money, all gone.

The hallway seemed to stretch out like a child's rubber toy, and the faster she hurried, the more her path seemed to dip away into the horizon. She bit her knuckles as she ran faster and faster toward Theodore's studio door. Could he still be there?

As she neared, Flora heard an enormous commotion from within. There was the crash of breaking glass. The horrifying rip of canvas and the sound of solid objects hitting the walls.

"Theodore!" Flora screamed, flinging open the door.

Flora gasped as she took in the room. The huge, stately studio, always Theodore's haven of tranquility, looked as if it had been trampled by wild animals. Paint had been flung onto the walls, and easels lay crumpled and broken on the floor. Paintings lay facedown on fragments of broken pottery. Everything—paintbrushes, oils, boxes of pastels—had been smashed to the ground.

As Flora entered, Theodore turned, and she could feel her heart rise up in horror. She'd seen him angry and tormented before. But the man standing in front of her was a Theodore completely transformed, as if his spirit had suddenly snapped with frustration, breaking the quiet of his mind.

She gasped, unable to believe that this was her husband standing before her. His dark hair stood up in sweaty clumps, and his skin was milky white beneath his stubble of beard. His white shirt was unbuttoned and torn, spattered with paint. Worst of all was the horrible, menacing look on his face, as if he were ready to destroy everything and everyone that meant something to him.

Flora drew back in shock. "What's wrong, my love?"

He turned and gave her an evil-looking, wide-mouthed smile, then grasped the small chair standing askew next to him. In a flash he picked up the chair and flung it carelessly through one of the studio's huge windows, smashing the glass into a thousand pieces.

Flora screamed as the night air rushed in. But Theodore just threw back his head and laughed.

"Stop!" Flora cried out in terror. What had happened to her husband? Had he gone mad?

She stepped closer, trying to reach him. But for each step she took, he took another one backward, his eyes gleaming cruelly at her, taunting her. At last he'd backed into a canvas that was propped in the corner of the studio, and he slowly turned around to face it.

Flora drew in her breath. The painting was

nearly complete, a full-length portrait of herself in a shimmering white gown. Theodore had painted it shortly after their honeymoon, and he had posed her in front of the roses that grew along their new home's long terrace. To Flora those long summer afternoons while Theodore painted her were the most precious time in their marriage.

But just as she was about to touch the back of his shoulder, Theodore suddenly reached for his belt and drew out a long, sharp hunting knife.

Flora opened her mouth in a mute scream. She watched in terror as he raised it high into the air and twisted it. Then with superhuman force he plunged the knife into the long, slender neck of her portrait, dragging the glinting knife sideways until the throat was completely slashed.

"No! No!" Flora screamed, horrified at watching her own image being mutilated before her eyes. What had happened to him? Why did he hate her so? Had she driven her husband crazy? Was it all her fault?

But Theodore acted as if he hadn't heard her screams. Silently, methodically, he picked up a small can of red paint and jimmied it open with the point of his knife. Then with a slow, deliberate motion he lowered the knife into the paint and drew it back out again, dripping red.

Flora drew her hands to her face in horror, unable to speak or move as Theodore took the knife and dripped the bloodred paint along the slash he had made in the portrait.

"Stop!" she screamed.

Again he dripped a line of red paint so that her beautifully painted neck appeared to be gashed open and pouring blood.

"Theodore!"

In one swift movement he turned toward her, dripping knife in hand, and pointed its tip to her own neck. His eyes, cold and green, seemed to glow from within. Sweat poured from his brow as he stepped closer and closer, the glinting point of the knife shaking only slightly as it moved toward her.

Flora finally screamed, long and low, as the room began to whirl and she felt her body slip noiselessly to the bare, hard floor. . . .

When Lila woke up, she lay curled up on her side, her hands clasped about her neck, her feet kicking the sheets. She opened her eyes in alarm.

What is happening to me?

Lila pulled her hands away from her neck and flipped over on her back, her heart racing. She gripped the side of the mattress as if it could keep her from spinning away. She was still breathing hard, and she could feel tears trickling down the sides of her face onto the silk pillowcase.

"Damon," Lila whispered, feeling the sobs well up inside her. "Damon, why is this happening?"

She wanted to tell Damon everything about her dreams. She'd wanted more than ever for him to understand. But she knew now that Damon had completely misunderstood what she'd said so far about her dreams. Had she really seemed that crazy to him? That . . . insane?

Lila bit her lip in fear. He had given her the strangest look yesterday in his office, as if he didn't believe a word she'd said. A wall had grown between them. His eyes, she remembered, were two green wells of fear and mistrust.

She felt her eyes drooping and fluttering closed, but as she did the phone suddenly rang, and she turned over to answer it.

"Hello?" she mumbled.

There was a short silence, followed by the sound of a male voice. "Lila?"

Lila frowned and wiped a stray remaining tear off her cheek. The voice sounded vaguely like Damon's, but she couldn't be sure. She squinted at her clock and saw that it was only five-thirty in the morning. "Yes? Who is this?"

Once again there was silence, but this time the silence was bone-chillingly long before her caller finally spoke. "Liiila," the voice sang, softly taunting her. "Liiila."

"OK, Damon," Lila snapped. "If you're calling to apologize to me, you're doing a lousy job."

There was a click on the other end of the line

before she'd finished speaking, and Lila hung up in disgust.

"If this is your idea of a joke, Damon, you're mean and you're sick." She lay back on her pillow, exhausted and drained—haunted by a new and inexplicable feeling that Damon could be playing with her. Taunting her. Driving her crazy.

Lila felt a deep chill go through her body. Maybe Damon knew much more about Theodore Grey than he let on. Maybe his life had become an obsession to him.

Could Damon actually be trying to duplicate the events of the painter's troubled life?

Lila instantly shook the crazy idea out of her mind. It was impossible. Exhausted and drained, Lila turned off her phone and buried herself under the sheets, praying for a deep, dreamless sleep.

"Flora!" she heard Theodore's voice roar over the sound of frantic, hollow footsteps. "Flora! *Flora!*"

His voice was drawing closer, and Flora sat up in bed, drawing the sheets up around her chin. A dull morning light shone through a crack in her drapes. She shivered, staring at the door to her room as the footsteps drew near.

There was a furious pounding at the door, and Flora bit her lip in terror as the doorknob began to twist back and forth. "Flora!"

After Theodore's tantrum last night she'd

rushed away and locked the bedroom door. But now, as she hurried toward the window, she wished she'd left the house altogether. There had to be someone who could help her.

Flora threw open the drapes and rushed onto the balcony, gripping the edge and leaning over, searching for a foothold. There had to be a way down into the garden. She had to get to safety.

"I need you right here, Flora!" Theodore's voice bellowed from the hall. She heard the insistent thump of his body smashing into the door and the splintering sound of the door's wooden frame as it began to break down.

I should have left last night, Flora thought desperately.

"Open this door!"

I should have run away and never come back.

"*Stand back!* I'm breaking down this door."

How can you do this to me, my love?

"Flora!" Theodore shouted. There was the sharp sound of ripping wood and the sickening squeak of nails coming out of boards. Flora pressed her back against the opposite wall just as the door broke open and swung crazily open on one hinge.

Theodore stood there, panting, his dressing gown soaked in sweat and covered with plaster and wood splinters. "Something has happened!" he panted. "You must come."

There was no escape. She had backed up onto

139

the balcony and was pinned against the railing now, the damp morning air stirring her hair and whipping her nightgown around her legs. He was walking slowly toward her, his face pale and wild. His long velvet robe was ripped and falling off one shoulder.

"What are you talking about?" Flora whispered, gripping the balcony railing.

As he drew near, Flora could see that tears had filled his eyes, but they didn't soften the ferocious expression on his face. "I'll show you what I'm talking about," Theodore said fiercely, grabbing her upper arm and pulling her away from the balcony into the bedroom and down the hallway.

"You're hurting me," Flora sobbed.

"You must have heard what was going on!" he cried, dragging her toward the door of the studio and flinging it open. "Why didn't you wake me?"

Flora stared. The studio looked exactly as it had the night before. Smashed canvases lay strewn over the floor amid puddles of paint and shards of glass from the broken window. She looked over at him, but his face was hard and accusing. "Why are you showing me this?"

His eyes blazed with fury. "What? Aren't you even a little bit shocked?"

Flora opened her arms. "I saw this last night. You did this yourself. You scared me to death."

"What are you talking about?" Theodore wailed, kneeling down and picking up a crushed painting he'd barely finished the week before. He held it in his hands, weeping.

"You were here, Theodore," Flora insisted. "Were you dreaming? I saw you with my own eyes."

He stood up slowly, his eyes burning. Then he swept his arm over the view. "You think I did this to *my own work?*"

"I saw you."

Theodore clutched his hair with both hands. "I've been working for two months to prepare for my next exhibition," he cried, picking up a piece of broken easel and throwing it back down to the floor. "Now every one of my pieces is ruined. You actually think *I* did this, Flora? How could you say such a thing?"

Tears poured from Flora's eyes. "But you were here," she pleaded. "You frightened me. . . ."

"I was asleep in the study at the other end of the house!" Theodore screamed, his eyes hardened with resistance. "Someone must have broken in. Didn't you hear? Couldn't you have awakened me?"

"Nooo!" Flora screamed, throwing herself into a chair and burying her face in her elbow. "Don't you understand? It's all so unbelievable and . . ." Flora finally gave up, dissolving into furious tears.

For the next few moments all Flora could feel was the dark, desperate interior of her mind swallowing her whole. Had she imagined her husband in the studio? Was he lying to her? Was she losing her mind?

When she finally opened her eyes, she realized

that Theodore was quietly beginning to pick his way through the debris. His eyes were now fixed on her portrait, which still stood in the corner of the studio, slashed and defaced.

The room was silent now except for the crunch of his shoes on broken glass and the rustling of the wind in the trees outside. Pale morning light began to rise through the windows.

"The portrait," Theodore was saying softly, reaching his hand out toward the nearly destroyed canvas.

"Look at it, Theo," Flora softly cried. "Look at it."

"Yes," Theodore whispered back, waving his hand back and forth in front of the slashed neck as if he were mesmerized. The red paint dripped horribly down her bust. "Fascinating."

Flora froze. "What did you say?"

"Fascinating," Theodore murmured, stepping back and leaning his head to one side as if he were considering a finished picture. "Compelling."

Flora opened her eyes wide with horror. "Theo . . . ," she warned.

"Yes," Theodore breathed.

"Theodore, you're not thinking of—" Flora broke off, unable to continue. The violent image sickened and repelled her.

"Yes," Theodore said dreamily. "I am. It will be the centerpiece of my exhibition. This piece right here."

Flora screamed.

Chapter Ten

Just thinking about her drives me crazy, Damon thought miserably, pushing away from his rolltop desk, standing up, and rubbing the back of his neck. *I can't get her out of my mind.*

It was late Friday evening, past ten o'clock, and his desk was finally clear. There'd been the last of his notes for next Monday's Renaissance art seminar. A recommendation for a graduate program. A little research on an obscure seventeenth-century painter that interested him.

A small fire was burning in his fireplace, and he collapsed onto the sofa in front of it, mechanically pulling the new novel he was reading off the side table and staring at it.

Lila.

He turned a page of the novel.

Lila.

A gust of wind knocked the side of the house and blew down the chimney, nearly putting out the fire. Damon thrust the book facedown next to him and looked into the struggling flames. He hadn't seen her since yesterday morning, and since then he saw her face every time he closed his eyes. He knew he'd been unforgivably horrible to her when she came to his office, distraught and needing his help.

But he couldn't explain why. What was wrong? Was Lila going crazy?

Or was he?

Damon stood up and paced in front of the fireplace. Something had come over him. It was a kind of coldness, as if a freezing chill had slipped in under his office door and enveloped him.

He shook his head. Maybe it was just the nervous state Lila had been in. Something always shut down inside him when he was around extreme emotions: anger, passion, hysteria. Especially hysteria. He was in the habit of guarding his heart. He had to. He'd always had to.

I've got to call her. I've got to at least tell her how sorry I am.

Damon continued pacing, mentally mapping out an apology, but somehow he couldn't seem to find the right words.

"Lila," Damon finally said out loud, picking up the phone and pretending to talk into it. "I— want to say—I'm sorry for not listening yesterday.

144

I—just wasn't myself," he stammered, dropping his hands to his sides and shaking his head. Slowly he put down the phone.

It's useless. I can't explain it.

He frowned and paced the room again, his mind a confused, jumbled space. Why couldn't he explain to Lila how it made him feel when she talked of eerie dreams and fantasies? She sounded as if she were deeply confused. Reality? Fantasy? Was she clear on which was which?

Slowly he walked to the far wall of his room, where he'd set up an oversize cork bulletin board for pinning up prints he wanted to study.

The night before, Damon had pinned several of Theodore Grey's later and most famous paintings, many of which were of his wife. Now he stood next to them, searching Flora's face for—

For what? Damon asked himself. A sign that Lila was telling the truth about her dreams? A sign that would tell him how he really felt about her?

Outside, the branches of a tree scraped against the window.

There was the large portrait Grey did of his wife, first, as the story went, as a conventional painting, right after they were married. Damon gazed at the curve of her cheek, the full lips, the teasing tilt of the eyebrow under the sweep of hair. Then he ran his finger down the line of her long, aristocratic neck, where the artist made the notorious bloody gash. His hand stopped, then pulled away suddenly as if the image were too painful to touch.

"This painting, like so many paintings of the surrealists," Damon began lecturing to himself in a soft, dreamlike voice, "shows the power of the subconscious mind below the surface of the painter's conventionality. He loves the beautiful woman but at the same time has an unconscious wish to destroy her. Creation exists beside death. Love next to hate. Real next to fantasy . . ."

Damon stopped midsentence, then stepped forward and stroked the image of Flora's bleeding neck with the tip of one finger.

"How could anyone damage such a beautiful neck?" he whispered.

Lila hurried toward the imposing front entrance of the university library. It was Friday night, and it looked as if the place was completely deserted, though a few lights still blazed from the dark building. The wind had picked up even more, and dark clouds raced across the face of the moon hanging over the campus.

Once inside, Lila headed directly for the main stairway to the second floor, glad that the place was nearly empty. She'd been distraught all day and definitely didn't want to run into anyone she knew. She'd barely had enough energy to throw on a hooded sweatshirt over a pair of leggings,

146

and her hair was pulled back in a messy ponytail.

That morning's eerie phone call had seriously frightened her, and her Flora nightmares were beginning to rub her nerves raw. Plus it definitely looked as if Damon had turned cold as ice on her.

Lila blinked back her tears. No matter how rotten things were between her and Damon right now, she knew she had to follow her own instincts. The dreams, after all, had taken on a life of their own in her mind. And now she had to find out what they were trying to tell her.

As she made her way toward the art stacks, only a few stragglers were left in the musty Western Research Room, and most of the study tables and carrels had been abandoned for the usual Friday night campus parties.

She was alone now, and she knew she had to face Grey's paintings, even though the thought of it terrified her. She had dreamed the ocean painting before she saw the real thing. What about the painting of Flora's neck—her own neck—slashed?

Lila shivered. Had that been real too?

In the art section she found the Theodore Grey book and grabbed several other surrealist volumes before heading for one of the empty tables. Her heart thumping, she slowly opened the book she'd glanced at only briefly the day before.

She stopped at one of the first pages she turned to and stared numbly at the image in front of her.

A sick, hollow feeling began to quake in her chest. There on the page, just exactly as it had appeared in her dream, was the portrait of Flora—her neck slashed and bleeding down the front of the canvas.

"How could he do that?" Lila whispered, disgust welling up inside her. "How could he do that to Flora?"

She bent down again to read the caption under the painting.

Grey's famous Woman as Death, *1937, was a sharp departure from his earlier works, in which the subject was almost always concealed within the boundaries of an inanimate object or scene. It is considered to be one of Grey's finest achievements, and because it represented a fresh new turn in his flagging career, his popularity soared once again. Still, scholars point to* Woman as Death *as a bizarre foreshadowing of the personal tragedy Grey endured shortly after it was first shown.*

"Bizarre foreshadowing?" Lila gasped. "What?"

Lila scanned the section in vain for more information, but neither the Theodore Grey biography nor the books on surrealism could explain the "personal tragedy" Grey suffered.

Lila rubbed her arms as if a chill had descended on her. As an afterthought she hurried downstairs to the reference librarian.

"May I help you?" the librarian asked in a brisk voice.

"Um, yes," Lila said softly, her throat beginning to swell with fear. "I'm looking for any articles written about a famous surrealist artist named Theodore Grey."

"Recent articles?"

Lila bit her lower lip. "No. Something further back. From . . . when he was alive. Say 1936, 1937."

The librarian's eyes gleamed with interest. "I'll need the name again and a general location of his residence."

Lila's heart beat faster. "Theodore Grey. I think he lived on Long Island, in New York."

"Mmmm. Let me show you our microfiche lab. We have copies of *The New York Times* dating back to 1898 and its biographical service on CD-ROM. So we should be able to come up with it."

Lila nervously followed the woman into a separate glassed-in area, where a dozen or so computers and microfiche machines were lined up on long tables. She closed her eyes as the librarian began typing at a keyboard.

Personal tragedy he endured? Lila thought with mounting terror. *What happened to him?*

"OK," the librarian said. "*The New York Times.* Uh-huh. We're looking for someone named Grey. *G-r-e-y?*"

"Yes."

"Grey, Theodore," the librarian went on, her fingers flying over the keyboard.

Lila watched as the librarian sat back. A few

moments later the screen blinked and several lines of print appeared. "Here we are."

Lila leaned over and scanned the screen.

"Grey home opened to lavish Long Island fete," The New York Times, *pg. 5, Sunday, September 5, 1936.*

"New Theodore Grey works revealed at down-town gallery gala, The New York Times, *pg. 14, Saturday, February 15, 1937.*

Grey, Flora. Obit. The New York Times, *pg. 115. Sunday, September 14, 1937.*

Lila gasped. Instinctively her hands flew to her throat. She felt as if gravity had ceased, as if she were flying at the speed of light toward a wall that was as vast and dark as infinity.

The librarian turned. "What's wrong?"

"Obit?" Lila said in a scared whisper. "As in obituary? *Flora Grey's* obituary? In *1937?*"

The librarian nodded. "Yes. Would you like to see the article? I'll show you how to use the microfiche," she said, pulling out a long narrow filing cabinet drawer filled with tiny envelopes. She held one up to the light. "Here we go."

Flora dead? Lila thought in horror. *That was the personal tragedy Theodore endured shortly after the slashed painting was exhibited?*

Lila felt sick. Her heart thumping in her chest, she followed the librarian to the microfiche machine. In a few moments she would learn how Flora died—and the thought terrified her.

The librarian settled herself in a chair, slapped a thin sheet of plastic on a glass, and carefully focused the viewfinder.

"Here it is," she said finally. "Obit for Flora Grey. And here are some related news articles in the same edition. Let me know if I can help you with anything else this evening."

"Thank you," Lila breathed, slowly sitting down in front of the machine, her eyes fixed to the screen, which had an enlarged projection of a newspaper headline that read: Famous Artist's Socialite Wife Found Dead at Long Island Estate.

Lila gulped. Two grainy black-and-white photographs stared out at her. There was Theodore, his high, handsome forehead and piercing eyes looking exactly like Damon's, though his dark hair was slicked back from his face. And there was Flora. Lila felt a dull, cold stabbing sensation in her chest—so painful, she could barely breathe. It was the face she recognized from the paintings. Yet it was hers as well.

Lila drew her hands up to her cheeks in horror. There were her own eyes looking back at her, as if they were staring at her from the dead.

Her eyes dropped down from the photographs, and she read until she saw something that made her stop breathing.

Long Island police say that Mrs. Grey suffered fatal wounds about the neck as a result of an attack at her home. According to police, Mrs. Grey's husband, the noted painter Theodore Grey, has been placed under arrest and is being considered the chief suspect in his wife's apparent murder. Neighbors alerted police to the scene after loud quarreling was heard in the vicinity of the couple's home.

Lila's face was going numb. She gripped the sides of the microfiche machine and stared at the words in horror.

"Theodore *murdered* Flora?" she cried softly. All she could think of were the horrible portraits of Flora, her neck slashed and dripping with blood. Theodore had slashed her image, then had taken the act into his real life?

She placed one hand over her mouth to muffle her sobs and with the other she pressed the make-copy button on the side of the machine.

Theodore and Flora. Damon and Lila.

Lila's head was swimming. She felt herself reaching back in time, backward through all the choices and circumstances that had led her to this spot in time. Then she closed her eyes and imagined the path extending back even before she existed. Long before. Until it reached another life so distant from hers and yet so identical that her life had become a mere echo of what had happened before.

Lila stood up as if in a dream, the copy of the

article clasped in her hand. She would show him. She had to show him. Flora and Theodore's faces. Their faces. Her dreams. Damon's obsession with Theodore's paintings. It all fit together. She had to tell him. She had to warn him before it was too late.

Her *own* life was at stake; she knew that now. And she was the only one who could save herself. She was the only person who knew what the future held.

Unless Damon already knew too.

Inside Damon's apartment the mood was restful. The small fire burned pleasantly, and the radio was tuned to a jazz station. He took a deep breath and continued reading the novel, a well-written mystery involving the theft of a famous painting.

Should he have called Lila to apologize? A part of him knew that he should have. Definitely. She was clearly upset. Yet he also knew that he needed some space around him right now—if only for a few hours.

Things were moving too fast: his teaching position, his intense feelings for Lila . . .

Damon shifted in his seat and looked into the fire. It had taken a long time for him to learn not to push things too quickly. He'd been the lucky one. He'd learned to temper his passion with time, reason, and even solitude. Now he knew in his heart that the good things were always worth waiting for.

He set his chin. If Lila cared about him, she'd have to understand that too.

He was about to pour himself another cup of tea when he heard a sudden pounding at the door. He froze. It was a wild, closed-fist pounding, like . . .

"You've got to let me in!"

Damon stood up and faced the door. "Lila?"

"Please!" he heard her cry out.

Damon hurried to the door and opened it. But when he saw Lila, something inside him collapsed. She looked like a pale fragile shadow of her former self. Her hair was scraped back off her face in a tangled ponytail, and her eyes were wild and red rimmed. Even her smooth, dusky voice had been replaced with high-pitched shrieks.

"Lila!" Damon said softly, pulling her in. "What is it?"

Her eyes were glued to his, as if she were pleading silently with him. Slowly she lifted a sheet of paper that she held, trembling, in her hand. "This."

He ignored the sheet of paper and closed the door. He shook his head as she waved it in front of him. "Yes. Yes, I'll look at it. But first—"

"Read it," Lila blurted. Her eyes seemed to burn into his. "Then tell me I'm imagining things about Flora and Theodore. *Read it!*"

Damon stepped back. He knocked away the sheet of paper reflexively so that it fell out of her hand and drifted down to the floor.

"You've got to," Lila whimpered, covering her

face with her hands. She slumped into a small chair next to the door.

Damon stood stiffly in place. "What are you talking about?"

"Theodore *murdered* Flora," she wailed. "And I was there. Or I was almost there. . . ."

Damon stared in disbelief. He could hardly believe that this distraught, ragged-faced woman in front of him was the same confident, beautiful woman he'd fallen in love with only a few days ago. It was clear she was having some pretty frightening dreams, but now it looked as if she were going through some kind of deeper emotional disturbance.

Lila suddenly stood up and grabbed his arms. "You *do* think I'm imagining things, don't you?

Damon looked closely into Lila's face and let his shoulders slump. "Yes, I do, Lila."

Her mouth tensed into a single line. She yanked her hands away from his arms in frustration and turned around.

"Lila," Damon said in a quiet voice. "Please try to get ahold of yourself. You're a beautiful, wonderful, fascinating woman and I . . . I think I've been falling in love with you, but I . . ."

Tears filled Lila's eyes as she leaned her head back to look up at him. "But what, Damon?"

Damon pushed down the frustration that was crawling up inside him like a wild animal. "But . . . ," he began carefully, "please try . . . please try to . . . to control yourself. I'm really worried about your . . . your emotional health right now and—"

Lila suddenly drew back. "You think I'm crazy!" she cried, nodding violently. "That's what Theodore told Flora. He told her that she was crazy, that he *hadn't* destroyed all his paintings *and it was him all along*—"

"Stop it!" Damon shouted. "Stop it! Stop it!"

Somewhere in the background he could hear Lila sobbing hysterically, but by this time he knew that something inside him had snapped and that he couldn't hold in his rage any longer.

"He hurt her! He threw things at her and threatened her with a knife!" Lila shouted.

"Is that what you *want,* then?" Damon cried, grabbing her and shaking her. Sweat poured off his face, and he could feel the muscles in his arms violently thrusting her back and forth. He felt strangely disconnected from his body. His rational mind was incapable of stopping the rage that had taken over.

Lila began screaming, but her screams only urged him on.

"Is that why you're telling me all these crazy stories?" Damon shouted. He grabbed a hunk of her hair and yanked her head back so that he could look directly into her terrified brown eyes. "Do you really think that I am Theodore and that you are Flora? Do you want me to hurt you the way you imagine *he* hurt her?"

Damon watched Lila's head shaking up and down like a rag doll's, but he couldn't stop. He shook her harder. "Should I beat you and threaten you with a knife now?"

Lila let out a long wail and beat his chest with her fists. "You're just trying to make me think I'm going crazy!"

"Should I beat you up? Would that prove you're right?" Damon shrieked. *"What do you want from me, Flora?"*

Lila continued to scream even after Damon stopped shaking her and bolted out of the room.

When she finally stopped, she closed her eyes and rested her head down on the carpet inside of Damon's front door. There was an eerie stillness in the empty air now, as if her struggle with Damon had sucked all the energy out. The only sound she could hear now was Damon's voice, suspended in her mind, calling her:

"Flora!"

Lila shuddered, then rose, bruised and sore, to her feet, hoping to leave as quickly as she could, without seeing Damon. But when she stood up, she saw that Damon was sitting in a chair by the fireplace, his head sunk into both hands.

She rubbed her arms and stepped forward, her mind too numb to say a word.

Slowly Damon lifted his head, and Lila saw

that his face was ashen. "I'm sorry," he said weakly. "I'm so sorry."

Lila knew that she should have left right then, without another word. But something made her turn her head slightly so that she had a view of the other end of the room. And what she saw sickened her to the core. The far wall had been plastered with Theodore's violently defaced paintings of his wife.

"You're insane!" Lila said suddenly, backing away, reaching for the doorknob behind her.

"Lila, please . . . ," Damon begged her, hands outstretched.

Lila's eyes widened. "How—could you?"

"What?"

A chill tore through Lila. "How could you—like looking at that? This painter—he terrorized his wife. He—murdered her. He—he wasn't an artist—he was a killer."

Damon got up and approached her, his eyes pleading. "Please, Lila. These paintings are historic works of art. I've been studying them for years."

"Then you're demented!" Lila shot back, twisting the doorknob. She knew she had to get away from him quickly.

Damon's face seemed to turn in on itself. He flushed red, then paled. "You don't understand. These painting are beautiful—"

"You're crazy!"

"I'm—not—crazy," Damon growled softly, stepping toward her.

Lila turned and jiggled the doorknob again.

"I hung those pictures up because they reminded me of *you!*" Damon said, his voice rising. "Don't you understand?"

"If *that*"—Lila pointed to the painting of Flora's gashed neck— "reminds you of *me,* then I definitely *don't* want to be anywhere near you, Damon."

"I can't let you go," Damon said in a low voice, moving toward her with careful steps.

"I'm sure that's what Theodore told Flora," Lila cried, "but I'm not going to stick around and let you murder me too!"

"Lila!" she heard Damon calling out as she flung open the door and rushed out into the windy, black night.

Damon clasped his forehead in frustration as he watched Lila's back recede into darkness.

What's wrong with me? She doesn't understand. She . . .

He turned on his heel, at a loss for an explanation—even to himself. Once in the bedroom he grabbed his suitcase out of the closet, then began yanking clothes out of his top dresser drawer.

"I've got to get out of here," Damon muttered to himself, pulling open another drawer. "Or—or I'm going to lose my mind."

He stiffened as the thought twisted its way through his head. Lose his mind? Sure, it could happen to him, given the right combination of love, confusion, and pressure. Couldn't it?

Look at what just happened with Lila, Damon told himself. *I started turning into another person. Someone vicious. Someone out of control. Someone unable to cope with another human being in need.*

He straightened up from his suitcase, his fists tightening into two hard knots. "I don't like this," he whispered. "There's no way I'm going to end up like . . ."

Damon cut off the thought almost before it had begun, then snapped his suitcase shut and swung it down off the bed. In the living room he picked up the phone to call Lila. He needed to leave town for a few days to cool his head. And even if she *had* completely written him off, he still wanted her to know.

But when he picked up the phone, he stopped himself.

If I talk to her now, if I hear her voice, I might change my mind. And I don't want anything to stop me from leaving town. Nothing.

"I'll call her from the airport," Damon muttered under his breath as he headed out of the bedroom, suitcase in hand.

Then, just as he was about to leave through the front door, something made him stop. Lowering his suitcase, he stepped back into the living room to look at the Flora painting one more time. His eyes fixed on the face, he walked slowly toward her, the only sound in the room coming from the fire's collapsing embers and the scraping of the branches against the building. He shivered. Her radiant face looked back at him with an amused seductiveness. Her bearing was aristocratic, but there was warmth and intelligence in the eyes that seemed to draw him in. . . .

Damon sank to the floor in front of the painting, his mind turning with confusion. He closed his eyes, and in his darkness he could see Lila's face. Flora's face. He imagined—as he had imagined so many times before—the inside of Theodore Grey's mind. The anger. The frustration. The horrible need to be recognized and loved and honored until it became the most important thing. More important even than his wife.

He opened his eyes and looked at the painting again. "I know you're trying to say something to me, Theodore," Damon whispered. "I know you want me to understand what you were going through."

Damon fell over on his side as the dark, anxious feelings began to wrap around his heart like a snake. He knew he had to get out of the house. He knew he had to breathe some fresh air, but he was paralyzed by the cramped and unbearable state of his mind.

Maybe she was right. Maybe I am losing my mind.

He stared at the painting. "Should I stay, my love? Or should I leave? Please tell me. *Please.*"

Chapter
Eleven

"Are you ready, dear?" Theodore asked. His eyes roamed over her beaded dress. "You look so lovely tonight."

"Yes," Flora replied. "Thank you."

She was staring out the window of the long, dark limousine as it slithered toward the bright lights ahead. There was the sound of muffled honks, taxi whistles, shouting and laughing in the street. When they stopped, she saw a glittering gallery entrance, framed by a silver awning and two uniformed doormen waiting on either side.

She felt him squeeze her hand and looked over. Theodore looked so handsome and gleaming in black tie, his wavy dark hair brushed back and his face flushed with anticipation. "Are you sure?"

Flora squeezed his hand back, hesitating. "I just wish . . ."

Theodore held up his hand and gently waved her words away. "Darling. This exhibition is a breakthrough for me. I *couldn't* show you the paintings first. I couldn't risk . . ."

Flora flinched. She knew what he was trying to say. He couldn't risk having her see them and refusing to come. But she *did* come, didn't she? She'd tried to forgive him for his horrible rampage in the studio and his bizarre denial that he'd ruined the paintings himself. She was going to stand by her husband, no matter what.

"Risk what, Theo?" she asked, her voice barely above a whisper.

"Come," Theodore said instead. "Think of the new dresses I'll buy you when we're done tonight. Think of how we'll make our home a palace again."

Flora shivered. She had no idea what he had prepared for this gallery opening. Or how he had pulled it off. His crazy, self-destructive spree had taken place less than two weeks ago. Since then he'd barricaded himself in his studio, and they'd barely spoken. On those rare occasions when he wasn't painting, he'd kept his studio padlocked tightly. Since all his works had been destroyed that horrifying night, she speculated that he had quickly painted some broad abstracts. Or perhaps he'd had other paintings, waiting in storage. . . .

Haunting her thoughts, however, was her last glimpse of Theodore in his studio, dribbling red paint from a slash in her painted neck.

"The money isn't important, Theo," Flora said urgently before breaking off. The limousine driver, who had been standing anxiously at attention outside, finally opened the door. She had to get out.

Now Flora floated up the carpeted entrance to the Arthur McGraw Gallery, lightly holding Theodore's arm as they passed through the doors toward the huge throng gathered inside.

"Mr. and Mrs. Grey!" someone called out. "May we have your picture, please?"

Flora smiled as the flash exploded in her eyes. Then another. Nearly blinded, she moved inside as Theodore began shaking hands and making introductions. In the background Flora could hear a dignified string quartet, and waiters in black and white offered her canapés and champagne from silver platters.

Her mood lifted, and she could feel her laughter bubbling up from the champagne.

"Theodore!" A man in a silk ascot tie approached in the confusion. "Five of the large paintings have been sold already—only fifteen minutes into the show! Your new collection is a smashing success."

"Wonderful, isn't it, darling?" Theodore asked her.

Flora nodded, standing on tiptoe. The gallery floor was too crowded for her to get a glimpse of her husband's new works. But as she moved forward with Theodore the throng began to part and the paintings came into view.

Flora stared. Then she put her hand to her mouth, to her throat, to her stomach, unable to believe what she was seeing. She felt that she was about to tip over, but Theodore caught her just in time, propping her up discreetly with his strong, suited arm.

There, right in front of her and hundreds of New York's finest society figures, was her full-length portrait, slashed and bloodied just as it had been the night Theodore destroyed his studio.

Flora's knees began to buckle. The crowd, she began to realize, had quieted—waiting for her reaction.

Holding her chin up stiffly, she shifted her gaze to the next painting, hoping for relief. But beside her slashed portrait was another painting Theo had done months ago at their stables. She froze. In the painting she stood by her favorite horse, Jesse, only now her hands and feet had been crudely chopped off, then thrown into space. Blood poured from the amputated limbs as streaks against the blue sky.

Theodore leaned his head close to hers. "That one is called *Helpless Woman,* darling," he said, whispering through a stretched smile. "Would you please smile and nod for these good people here and break this terribly awkward silence?"

Flora felt a rush of tears, but something made her shake them off. What was it? Pride? Her need for the privacy of her feelings? Her refusal to let her humiliation show? *Maybe all three,* Flora thought, her mouth stretching into a horrible smile.

"How does it feel to be the star of your husband's new paintings, Mrs. Grey?" a reporter suddenly asked, popping in front of her while another camera flash popped.

"How does it feel to have your husband at the pinnacle of success in the art world?" another asked.

Flora's heart was breaking as she threw back her head with laughter and took a long sip of champagne. "Wonderful, darling! My husband's a genius, don't you think?"

There was a noticeable murmur of relief from the crowd.

"Six more sales, Theodore!" the man in the ascot cried out, waving a handful of order slips.

There was another explosion of light as another picture was taken. Flora could feel her husband grip her around the waist and murmur into her ear: "Isn't it thrilling, dear? We've got the world at our feet now."

Flora felt a wave of dizziness. *Yes, but at what price, Theo?*

"My sanity!" Lila called out, sitting up in bed.

She looked around her dark bedroom, then let her tense shoulders slump in frustration. Another dream. Another horrible dream.

She propped her elbows on her raised knees,

166

then raked her sweaty hair back with her hands. The dreams weren't going to leave her alone, were they? It was as if Flora's spirit still existed, suspended in time and space, and she was trying desperately to send Lila a message.

A warning.

Lila shivered, then jumped when the ringing phone suddenly pierced the silence of her thoughts. She picked it up and cautiously put the receiver to her ear.

"Li-la?" a voice asked.

Lila shivered. The voice. The same singsong voice that reminded her strangely of Damon's. Was it because she'd just awakened from another Theodore dream? Or was it . . .

"Liiila?"

Her bottom lip began to tremble, and she quickly hung up. Was there something seriously wrong with her mind? Lila turned over in bed and punched her pillow into place, struggling to think objectively. Logic would tell anyone that the calls were probably just a bunch of stupid kids pulling pranks at a slumber party.

Yet part of her wanted to believe the calls were somehow tied up with the mystery of her dreams. The dream of Theodore, then his voice—or Damon's voice—on the phone, taunting her. How could it be otherwise?

Rrriiiinnnggg.

Lila's eyes widened. She turned and stared at the phone, fear welling up inside her. She knew she was crazy to pick up the phone again, but somehow she couldn't help herself. . . .

"Flo-ra?" the same voice asked softly. "Flooora."

Lila felt a wrenching sensation in her chest, as if the wind had been knocked out of her. Then she gasped and slammed the phone down in horror.

"No!" she sobbed, grabbing the phone. With shaking hands she tried several times to punch the ringer off before it finally disconnected. She threw herself facedown on her bed, beating the pillow with her two fists.

Was she going crazy? Was she hearing things? Was she making this whole thing up in her mind? Was Damon right? Should she start worrying about her *emotional health*?

Or was he deliberately trying to make her worry about it?

Who could have known about Flora? Lila thought. She racked her mind for a memory. Had she talked to Jessica about her dreams? Isabella? Someone at the library?

Lila shook her head, sickened. No. There was only one person in the world who knew of her interest in Flora Grey.

And that was Damon.

*   *   *

Flora seemed to be floating through her long, lovely hallways. Her silken slippers made no sound as they touched the endless velvety carpets. And as she passed each tall window she let her hand caress the sumptuous draperies that had been hung only recently, spilling in shiny pools where they reached the floor.

She sighed, glancing at her reflection as she passed another tall mirror. Her blue dressing gown of priceless Chinese silk, slippery against her legs, shimmered in the dim light.

"So far to go," Flora murmured as the hallway intersected with another. She looked up and down the rows of golden doors. "Why can't I remember which way?"

Still, the walk was very beautiful, she had to admit, wherever it led her. She heard music in the distance, pulling her forward, though she paused to admire the paintings along the way: the brilliant van Goghs, the lush Renoirs, the melting watercolors.

Theo's paintings paid for all this, Flora told herself. *However cruel I thought he was for showing them, they have brought us such wealth and security.*

"At last," Flora whispered to herself as a large swinging door appeared before her at the end of the corridor. She pushed through it and realized it was the kitchen she had been trying to reach for so long. It had been impossible to sleep, even with

Theo resting so peacefully next to her. Perhaps some warm milk would help.

She glided toward the refrigerator and found a small bottle of milk. The kitchen was so large now, she thought, even though it had taken so long to rebuild. She was nearly lost among the brand-new steel counters, the walls of cupboards, and the huge chopping board in the room's center, bristling with its rows of waiting knives. She and Theo needed their new kitchen now for their new fleet of chefs and the large dinner parties they were giving.

Milk bottle in hand, Flora searched the cabinets for a pan to heat it in.

There was a slight sound to her right. But such a slight sound, she thought. She couldn't let herself be so afraid anymore. All was well now. All was well.

Then suddenly Flora's whole body jerked. She felt a hand on her arm, squeezing, then the milk bottle flying, smashing against the edge of the metal stove.

Suddenly, whirling from behind her, she saw the face of her attacker. Flora gasped. Was it Theodore? His eyes were wild and dark. His face—so changed, like an animal's. She remembered so vividly this face from the night he'd destroyed his paintings in the studio. And yet she hadn't seen him like that for months. Now he looked even more savage than before.

He destroyed his paintings that night. Will this be the night he destroys me as well? Flora thought with terror.

"Theodore?" Flora cried. "Theodore, what's happened?"

His awful face dipped down, and Flora felt the brute strength of his arms grasping her waist. There was the sensation of being lifted into the air, then being thrown, loose and shuddering, across the room until the side of her body hit the wall and smashed to the ground.

Sharp pain broke through her daze. The side of her face stung, and her shoulder throbbed. She opened her eyes, unable to move, her right cheek flattened into the floor. A trickle of drool began to spill out from the corner of her mouth.

"Look at you," she heard Theo's voice taunting her.

Flora opened her mouth to speak. "Theo?" she whispered in a cracked voice.

She watched as his face dropped down next to hers, cracked in two by its wide, giddy grin. "Yeeesss? What is it, Flora? Is something *wrong?*"

Flora stared, her body racked with pain. Ten minutes ago Theo had been sleeping peacefully at her side. What had happened to him? Had he fallen into another insane, artistic rage, like the night he had destroyed his studio?

"What is it, Flora?" he shouted into her ear.

"What—have—I—done?" Flora whispered, her voice breaking. A stabbing pain shot through her jaw.

"You took my ideas!" Theo shouted. "Then

you took the money people gave you for my ideas and kept it for yourself!"

Flora closed her eyes in confusion. "What—what are you—talking about, Theo? They were *your* ideas, my darling. You're not well. You're—"

"Shut up!" he threatened, his voice high above her now. "You took everything from me. You left nothing. And now you owe me, Flora."

"Owe you," Flora echoed. She opened her eyes halfway, but the room began to spin and heave. "I owe—you—what?"

There was the slight sensation of his head dipping down next to hers, and when she opened her eyes again, she saw the full view of his face again, so pale and ill. "You owe me with your life, Flora. Your *life*."

Lila's eyes flew open. Her back was soaked with perspiration and sticking to her silk sheets. She moaned out loud, the awful memory exploding in her pounding head.

"I can't take it," Lila wailed softly, trying to sit up, then sagging back onto the pillow. Her dream life was deteriorating as badly as her waking life was.

"And there's nothing I can do about it," Lila whispered softly, wiping back the tears trickling down her cheeks. "Except try to live my life as normally as I can."

Lila slowly rose from bed. Her meeting last night with Damon was too unbearable to contemplate.

It was true that she'd been upset—actually, completely distraught and out of control. But the way he'd reacted to her distress was . . .

"It was unforgivable," Lila said out loud. She stood and looked down at the bruises that covered her sore wrists and forearms. "And it's over, Damon. It's over between us."

Lila padded into her bathroom, turned on the shower, and stepped in quickly, letting the hot water massage her shoulders and back. After that, she squeezed some of her most expensive shampoo into her hands and worked it thoroughly into her hair.

She took her time making up her face, even breaking into the new stash of French cosmetics she'd bought at an exclusive boutique the week before. Her pale face brightened. Her eyes, swollen and pink, began to sparkle. Even her dry, cracked lips were starting to shine.

Lila walked slowly into her living room and sat down. She stared quietly at the oil painting over the fireplace.

"I thought I loved you, Damon," she whispered. "I thought I could trust you and share my life with you. I thought . . ." Lila struggled to continue, her voice cracking with emotion. "I thought that you cared."

Lila walked miserably back into her bedroom and turned her phone ringer back on. Then she punched the messages button on her answering machine, sat down on the edge of her bed, and stared sadly out the window.

"I'm Lila Fowler, and we Fowlers don't let things or people push them around," Lila made herself say as her messages began to play. "It's not in our genetic structure."

The messages began, and Lila listened carefully. "There's a hang-up," Lila muttered. "And another hang-up. And another." She forced herself not to react. The machine beeped again, and Lila was suddenly listening to Damon's voice.

"Hi, Lila."

She bit her lower lip. He sounded so tired and dejected.

"I'm at the airport . . . and I just wanted you to know that I'm leaving town for a couple of days. I know I behaved badly, Lila, and that you need my support right now. But I have to get away and let things cool down. Too many strange things are happening, and they're getting between us. I—I'll call you when I get back. Take care, Lila."

There was a beep as the message ended, and Lila flopped backward on her bed, her eyes smarting. She could almost see his face in front of her. His lips, warm and firm. She remembered every detail of their first date together, just a little over a week ago. The quiet table at Andre's, the shy way he took her to his apartment and eagerly showed her his pictures and books. The fiery kisses on his couch.

Maybe I've been unfair, Lila thought. *Maybe Damon isn't the crazy, volatile Theodore of my dreams. Maybe there was a reason for the way he acted last night.*

Lila slowly began to consider the possibility that she could end up losing someone she could be happy with. Someone she'd never be able to find again in her life.

She took a deep breath and looked out the window. Light flickered in her courtyard's spreading trees, and the darkness of the past few stormy days had momentarily lifted.

The phone rang suddenly, and Lila immediately answered it, hoping it was Damon. There was so much she wanted to tell him.

"Hello? Damon?"

There was a brief silence on the line, followed by a far-off noise she couldn't immediately place. "Damon? Is that you?"

The noise got louder until Lila realized it was someone chuckling softly into the phone. The laughter got gradually louder until it turned into an eerie, high-pitched cackle that made Lila immediately wish she'd screened the call.

"Who is this?" Lila demanded angrily.

"Your boyfriend's gone now, isn't he?" the voice crackled into the phone. "He can't help you anymore."

Lila stopped breathing.

"Too bad, Liiila."

Lila slammed down the phone. For a moment she just sat there, fighting the urge to scream. Her thoughts were spinning in her head, and she had to fight to control them. Who else would have known that Damon had left town? A friend? Someone in the art department? The same person had to have known about her Flora dreams. But she hadn't told anyone but—but *Damon*.

Damon.

Could it be possible that Damon was actually playing a cruel game with her?

Lila set her jaw. She was going to find out once and for all who was making the calls. Before another minute passed, she was going to get into her car, drive to a home electronics store, and buy a caller ID machine.

Chapter
Twelve

An hour later he was waiting in his car outside Zap Communications in downtown Sweet Valley. He'd been looking for Lila, with no luck, until he spotted her red Miata at an intersection near her apartment.

There was so much they needed to talk about. He'd never felt quite so confused before about anyone. What did she want? How could they work things out so they could be together—for always?

His mind sifted back through their relationship, though so many of the details were hazy now. What was it that made her so angry last night at his apartment? He had to talk to her right away so she could clear things up for him.

He dropped his head until his forehead was resting on the top of the steering wheel. So many things. They made his head hurt so.

There. There she is. She's coming out of the store

now, carrying a—what's in that plastic bag?

He straightened in his seat to get a better look. She looked so beautiful today! Her thick hair was fluffed about her shoulders, its silky strands shooting rays of light. So bright! Today she was wearing pink and her dress was short, showing off her long, slender legs. He sighed. Lila was the only woman in the world he'd ever be able to love.

As he got out of the car he tried to think. There had been an argument. He should apologize. Yes. That would be the first thing.

"Lila!" he said, mustering his most confident voice.

She stopped and turned around. He could see her lips part, as if she were about to say something and didn't. He neared and was finally close enough to take in the silky smoothness of her skin. The beautiful white neck and long, tapered hands.

"Damon? I thought you'd left town." She took another step toward him, and he could see her eyes traveling over his clothing. She was hesitating, he could tell. Maybe even afraid. She pulled her purse strap higher on her shoulder.

He reached out his hand for her. "I couldn't leave."

A car honked. Pedestrians, bicyclists, and a woman with a baby stroller all passed them by as they stood there in the middle of the busy sidewalk, staring at each other.

"I see," Lila said simply. He could see hurt in her eyes. What had happened?

He cleared his throat. "Lila. I . . ."

She looked a little confused. "What is it?"

He looked down into her soft brown eyes. So lovely and pleading. "I just wanted to say that I'm sorry. Sorry for everything."

"You already apologized—on the phone," Lila told him, her eyes flickering with fear. Was it fear?

"Well, I wanted to tell you in person," he said quickly. "That's why I decided at the last minute not to leave town."

Yes. Of course. That was the reason I didn't leave.

Lila let her shoulders fall, and he could hear a small sigh whispering from between her lips. "I don't know what to think anymore. Last night was terrible. You frightened me. You let me down."

"I know."

Lila lifted her face to his. "You hurt me last night." Tears flooded her eyes. "I don't let people treat me like that."

He pulled her in, and he could feel her body soften as she gave him the briefest embrace. A thrill shuddered through him. Her touch was almost too much for him to bear.

A group of passing students whistled, and he gently pulled away, slipping his arm around her waist and leading her to her car.

"Let's go have some coffee and talk," he suggested. "Do you have some time?"

Lila looked up at him when they stopped in front of the Miata. She seemed to take in his face, as if she were examining every pore. For a split second he was sure she was going to turn him down.

But then her lips curved into a small, scared smile. "OK," she finally said. "Coffee. That sounds good."

"Like I said, Lila. I'm really sorry about everything."

Lila looked uncomfortably into Damon's eyes as she sipped her coffee. Still fresh in her mind was the rough way he had grabbed her and shaken her the night before. She was bruised, frightened, and upset. How could he possibly explain that away?

She bit her lower lip and let her eyes drift away. The restaurant he'd led her to was a dimly lit greasy spoon, which was nearly empty except for a few men smoking cigarettes and drinking coffee at the counter.

He seems so tired, Lila thought. His eyes, usually so bright with curiosity, were dull. Even his voice sounded flat, as if all the emotion had been drained out of it. And what had he done to his hair? Tried to cut it himself?

He's probably as wiped out as I am by this whole thing, Lila thought as she nervously rolled the edge of her paper napkin.

"Lila?" Damon prompted her, catching her gaze.

"Oh. Yes," Lila stammered. "Maybe it's not a good time for me to talk. These horrible dreams have me a little on edge."

His eyes seemed to urge her on.

Lila bit her lower lip. "A *little* on edge. Ha. That's an understatement. I can barely sleep." She paused. "And now . . . well, now there's another problem. Something I haven't told you about."

He reached for her hand and squeezed it. "What is it, darling? Why haven't you told me?"

Lila shrugged and gently pulled her hand away. "It's too weird. And I've already burdened you with enough."

"Go on. You can tell me now."

Lila glanced around the room. In the distance the cash register dinged. A large, squabbling family was being seated at a booth near theirs. Then she looked down at the table. "I've been getting strange phone calls."

His eyes widened. "What? What kind of calls? Were they threatening?"

Lila nodded, then sipped her coffee. "But at first the caller just said my name. Only it was the *way* he said it. It was sort of like a taunt. It was . . . very spooky."

He sat back. "Is that all?"

Lila cupped her hands around her coffee mug, shaking her head. "No, that's not all. The caller called me Flora once."

He shrugged. "Must be some frat boy trying to give you a bad time."

Lila let her gaze travel back up to Damon's face, and she felt a chill. He looked distracted, as if he didn't even care about the caller and wanted to talk about something else. "But how did the same person know you were leaving town?"

Damon looked confused.

Lila leaned forward. "You must have told *someone* you were planning to leave town because the caller knew it. He said, 'Your boyfriend's gone now; he can't help you anymore.' I got that call right after I listened to your message from the airport."

Damon looked up to the ceiling as if he were searching for an explanation.

"That's why I bought this caller ID machine," Lila explained, gesturing toward her shopping bag. "I want to find out who's calling me."

His eyebrows shot up. "Don't you think you're carrying this a little too far?"

Lila's mouth hardened into a line. Damon still wasn't taking her seriously. He hadn't taken her seriously last night, and he certainly hadn't changed since then. In fact, he was starting to make her mad all over again. "No, I *don't* think I'm carrying it too far, as a matter of fact."

"It's probably a random crank caller," Damon insisted. "Anyone can call a woman on the phone and tell her they know their boyfriend's gone.

That tactic would probably work fifty percent of the time on any given day."

"But he called me Flora—"

"Those caller ID devices," Damon interrupted, pointing to Lila's shopping bag, "are a waste of money. I'm sure most of those crank callers call from phone booths anyway."

Lila shifted uncomfortably in her seat. A part of her mind wanted to start the whole conversation over again. After all, maybe she had pushed Damon too far.

Maybe he couldn't handle it.

"If you'd rather not talk about it," Lila said quietly, "I'll understand."

"I *don't* want to talk about it," Damon said flatly, reaching across the table to take her hand.

Lila felt a chill. His hand, so cold. She looked into his eyes. Something so odd. Maybe she'd never noticed it before, but there was a dullness to them. . . .

Then again, Lila thought sadly, *maybe I just imagined how bright his eyes were when we first met. I was so completely infatuated by him.*

"Lila? What's wrong?"

Lila felt something collapsing inside her. Had her heart stopped beating? Why did she keep feeling as if something wasn't quite right? How tired and confused was she anyway?

Suddenly Lila drew her hand away and started to get up from the booth. "I—I'll be right back," she said in a rush.

"Lila!" Damon demanded. "Sit down. Where are you going?"

Slowly Lila sat down, feeling more uncomfortable than ever. "I—I'm not sure, Damon. I just need to get home now."

His lips stretched into a smile. "You're not well. It's the only explanation, Lila. Let me take you home."

Lila gripped her purse strap. "No," she said abruptly. "I've got my car parked outside."

His face relaxed into a pout as he leaned forward on his elbows. "OK. But just one kiss before you go. I want things to be OK between us now, Lila. Please."

Slowly, gingerly, Lila leaned her face forward until her lips were pressing on his. For a moment her mouth hung there, as if it were weighted down by the sheer lack of desire. Then she pulled back, her eyes widening with fear. What had happened? His kisses had always made her feel like he had set off a thousand shooting stars inside her body. This kiss had made her feel like . . . nothing.

Damon, however, had a dreamy smile on his face.

Lila stared.

"Oh, Lila," he murmured, his eyes still closed, his face still hovering over the middle of the table.

Lila looked sharply at his face, then ran her finger along his right eyebrow. "That scar," she said. "I never noticed it before."

His face fell as he sat back.

184

Lila suddenly sensed that he was hiding something. She didn't know what. She didn't know why. "Come to think of it, there are a *lot* of things I don't know about you, Damon."

He narrowed his eyes. "What do you mean?"

Lila took a sharp breath. "I don't know anything about your family. I don't know your middle name. And I don't even know your phone number."

His face flushed an angry red. "You don't know what you're saying!"

Lila stood up, indignant. "I know exactly what I'm saying."

"Stop."

"On our first date, Damon," Lila went on, unfazed, "I told you what I learned when I lived away from home for so long, in Italy. Do you remember what that was?"

He looked up at her and cleared his throat nervously. "Well, yes, of course I remember."

Lila stared at Damon, the sadness and frustration mounting in her heart. How could this man sitting in front of her be the same man she'd connected with so powerfully the first day they met? She'd had so much hope. There'd been such a feeling of warmth and belonging. She felt now as if her heart had been shattered.

"I told you," she went on sadly, "that I learned to open my mind and trust my instincts. And right now I'm going to go with my instincts, Damon.

I'm going to leave. I don't think this relationship is a good one for either of us."

"Lila, wait," she heard Damon's voice calling her from behind, but she was out the door before she could hear another word of protest.

Lila hurried down the sidewalk, glancing over her shoulder to make sure Damon wasn't trying to follow her. When she reached her car, she unlocked it quickly and threw her purse and package in the passenger seat.

Fueled by a strange need to get as far away from Damon as possible, she instantly started the car, slipped on a pair of dark glasses, and zoomed off in the direction of her apartment.

Just settling into the familiar, buttery leather of her seat made her feel slightly better. But her stomach was still quaking. All she wanted to do now was get home and lock the door.

He didn't even seem to know me, Lila thought bitterly. *It was like talking to a stranger—except the stranger looked exactly like someone I loved.*

"Or thought I loved," Lila said softly, her eyes flooding with tears.

But I can't make my heart feel something it won't.

Lila brushed away the tears with her hand and shook out her hair in the breeze. It was going to be very hard to get Damon out of her mind, especially since everything had started out so beautifully. She flashed on the first time she'd seen him in class and how she'd instantly . . .

Lila stopped at a stoplight and frowned. Actually he'd been sort of obnoxious to her that first time in class. As a matter of fact, he'd made her feel like a complete fool.

"You'd better put that in your notes if you're taking any. . . ."

She bit her lip. She'd hated that moment. He'd singled her out, and everyone in the class had been laughing at her! *What's more,* Lila thought, stepping on the accelerator when the light turned green, I *was the one to approach him for a date, not the other way around.* He wouldn't give her his phone number even though he clearly had a phone. He didn't have the money to pay for their first date. And after that he didn't even call her for nearly five days!

Plus, Lila thought with a shudder, *he actually knocked me out cold with that book. Did he do that on purpose?*

Lila banged her hands on the steering wheel. "How could I have been so stupid?"

She shivered. Her mental list went on and on. What about Damon's weird fascination with Flora's image—a woman who was violently murdered by the man she loved? A woman who just happened to look like her!

"But he wasn't ever really interested in Flora," Lila thought out loud, her mouth trembling. "He

187

was just obsessed with her image. He never wanted to hear about my dreams or hear about what her life was *really* like."

Lila shuddered as she thought about the night he grabbed her and shook her and actually called her Flora.

He probably picked me out of the crowd because I looked just like Flora Grey—the sicko.

Suddenly Lila felt scared and vulnerable. She sighed with relief when she arrived safely home, but as she parked her car in her private garage in the back of her complex, she found herself taking special care to look over her shoulder.

She hurried inside her apartment, her caller ID device tucked under her arm. Then after she closed the door, she locked it securely, savoring the dim, orderly silence of her familiar surroundings. The muted, tasteful tones of her comfortable furniture and European antiques. The soft Persian carpets. The lovely painting over the fireplace. Lila sighed.

There was a sudden clicking sound in the kitchen, and she jumped. She put her hand on her heart, looked around slowly, then sagged with relief when she realized it was only the refrigerator kicking on.

Her heart thumping, she took the caller ID device out of the box and headed down the dark hallway toward her bedroom. It took only a few minutes to hook it up to her phone, but by the time she was done, her hands were trembling.

Lila sat down on the bed, twisting the hem of her dress. She detested the idea that anyone at all could harass her over the phone and that she had been forced into playing spy.

And yet . . .

She heard a thump against the side of her apartment. Then a split second later the phone suddenly rang, and she jumped.

Lila covered her mouth with one hand and ran out of the room into the hall. A chill shot through her, then a dull, dizzying fear that almost made her lose her bearings. The hallway seemed to stretch out before her, then shrink again. The phone kept ringing and ringing in her ears. She reached up and covered them with her hands. And as she closed her eyes all she could see was a foggy vision of an opulent hallway, lined with paintings. There were footsteps behind her, and she could almost smell the metallic tang of a steel blade, so close to her neck. . . .

"I've got to get out of here!" Lila gasped, opening her eyes and flinging herself down the hall. She got ready to leave, grabbing her purse and digging shakily for her keys. With trembling hands she hurried outside and locked the front door behind her. Then she turned around and bolted for her car in the back parking garage, sticking her key in and yanking open the door.

"Please start, please start," she begged,

pumping the accelerator. The car jumped backward. She spun the wheel and stepped on the pedal again, screeching out of the parking garage and back out into the windy afternoon.

The wind whipped Lila's hair as she roared down the quiet street, then out onto the highway that led to the coast. She pressed her back into the leather seat, stretched her left arm out straight against the steering wheel, and shifted into fifth. The car's engine purred, and the scenery streaked by in a blur.

Lila didn't know how long she drove before she started wondering what her next move would be. She hit the freeway into the city, then turned north up the stormy coastal highway, passing every car and truck in sight. To her left the blue-gray ocean stretched out smooth as a bowl under a churning, cloudy sky. The cliff-side mansions stood solid under swaying groves. The air tasted of salt, and her skin began to tingle as the first rains beat wildly against her windshield.

Finally her fear started to loosen. She could feel her wild heart slowing down. She turned onto a viewpoint that looked over the ocean and stared out to sea through the soothing back and forth of her windshield wipers.

I can't go home.

Lila tried to think as the coastal wind whistled about the car. She could go home to Fowler Crest, of course. But her parents were in Europe, and she didn't want to be alone. Bruce was in Japan. . . . Jessica?

Lila felt a flood of guilt. Jessica was the only one she wanted to be with right now, and yet she'd allowed Damon to come between them. She knew Jessica would help her—if she hadn't let Damon make fun of her like that in the lecture hall.

Lila banged the steering wheel again in frustration. *She'll probably never speak to me again. I didn't even come to her defense!*

She shuddered, wondering if that move with Jessica had been calculated as well. People without friends were always more defenseless than people with a strong support group.

He was probably trying to cut me off from my friends . . . so I'd have no one to turn to when he made his move!

Panicked, Lila started the engine and pulled back onto the highway, heading back to Sweet Valley. Her head was foggy again, her thoughts drifting crazily back and forth between Flora and Theodore and Damon and Lila. Maybe she *was* going crazy.

But one thing she was sure of now. She needed to talk to Jessica right away. And she hoped against all hope that Jessica would forgive her— because she had no one else to turn to.

"What are *you* doing here?" Jessica asked as soon as she opened her dorm-room door. Hand on her hip, she glared at Lila.

191

Though Jessica's blond hair had been carefully blown dry, Lila noticed that Jessica only wore a pair of gray athletic shorts and an oversize T-shirt. It was clear that Jessica had absolutely no plans for the day, even though it was a Saturday afternoon. Lila's heart expanded. She knew Jessica hated being stranded in the dorms on a weekend with nothing to do.

"I'm sorry, Jessica," Lila said softly. "I just needed to talk. Can I come in?"

"I'm right in the middle of—um—*something*," Jessica said instantly, her blue-green eyes flashing. "I do *not* have time for this interruption."

Lila looked over Jessica's shoulder. Soft music was playing, and the smell of nail polish was in the air. Jessica was clearly alone with zilch to do. "Please, Jessica."

Jessica looked Lila up and down. "You look terrible, Lila. I don't think that new boyfriend of yours is good for you."

Lila had to bite back the urge to contradict her friend. It was one thing to admit to yourself you'd made a stupid mistake. But quite another to admit it to a friend. Especially a friend who was boiling mad at you.

Lila lowered her head in shame, pressed her lips together, and nodded, tears springing to her eyes. "I'm so sorry, Jessica. Damon shouldn't have spoken to you like that in the lecture hall . . . about your attendance record . . . right in front of me. It was wrong."

Jessica drummed her fingers on her hip, not moving her icy stare. "You didn't exactly jump to my defense, did you?"

Lila looked down at her feet. She wanted desperately to run away but knew there was no place she could run away *to*. She *had* to make Jessica understand. "No," she finally said in a whisper. "I let you down."

There was a long pause. "Mmmm," Jessica finally said. "So now you're having problems with Mr. Lowlife, aren't you?"

Lila looked up and nodded. "I'm in big trouble, Jessica. I'm not seeing him anymore. And I really need your help right now."

Jessica's sour face instantly brightened. "If I forgive you, do you promise to take me for an entire weekend of fun at the Casa Mia Spa up in Napa Valley? I just read about it. It's the hottest, most exclusive, most *expensive* spa in California."

A smile began to form at the corner of Lila's mouth, and it felt very good. "Of course. We'll work on our tans, have a massage—"

"And a facial. Plus a mud bath and some underwater yoga . . ."

Lila nodded. "And we'll finish the whole thing off with fabulous dinners in the evening."

"Next weekend."

"Next weekend. I promise. We'll fly up to San Francisco, rent a car, and drive north to Casa Mia."

Jessica dropped the hand from her hip and opened the door wider. "OK. I *suppose* you could come in."

"Thank you." Lila sighed as she walked in and settled on Jessica's disheveled bed. It was such a relief to be with Jessica. Jessica didn't mince words with her, and that was a quality Lila was starting to appreciate.

Jessica shrugged, sitting down next to her and picking up her bottle of nail polish. "I have to admit, I was jealous. The guy is a total hottie."

Lila grimaced.

Jessica drew her knees up and squinted at her baby toe. "Oh, whatever. All's well that ends well."

Lila shook her head miserably. "It's worse than that, Jessica. Much worse."

Jessica sat up, her eyes brightening. "Really? Oooh. Spill! I want to know everything. Every little teensy-weensy detail."

Lila felt sick. The last thing she wanted to do was dredge up the whole story. But she knew she didn't have a choice. "I don't even know where to begin. It's such a strange, strange story. But I'll try to tell you as best as I can. . . ."

By the time Lila was done with her story, Jessica realized that her mouth had actually dropped open. "That is the most incredible story I've ever heard."

"Yes," Lila said tiredly.

Jessica's eyes were burning with interest.

"What an incredible psychic connection you had with him! You and Damon actually *look* like the painter and his wife. *You* are living her life in your dreams. *He* had been fascinated with Flora's face for so long. It's too spooky!"

"Anyway," Lila concluded, stretching out on Elizabeth's bed. "Now I don't know what to do. I've got this strange feeling that he's obsessing on Theodore Grey's abuse of his wife."

Jessica's eyes widened. "And when he sees you, he sees Flora. Creepy."

Lila nodded. "You're telling me. I keep thinking that maybe Damon's some kind of frustrated artist. Maybe somewhere in his past a woman got in the way of his work, like he imagined Flora got in the way of Theodore's work."

Jessica wrapped her arms tightly around her knees. "Whoa. I get the shivers just thinking about it. Did he actually *murder* Flora?"

Lila paled. "I think so."

Jessica felt queasy inside. "And then of course your dreams match up with the real story. And he was about to kill Flora in your dream, wasn't he?"

Lila stared. "You know, Jessica, sometimes I wonder how you manage to keep your GPA so low. You're really very bright."

Ignoring her, Jessica jumped up and sat down next to her friend. "There's got to be something we can do."

Lila rubbed her eyes and looked up. "The first thing I'm going to do is never see Damon Price again, even if it means dropping my lecture."

Jessica nodded. "Yeah. Then you have to get your life back to normal. Maybe that will put an end to all of these crazy dreams. We should go out this weekend. Go to a party. Hang out with the Thetas. Get makeovers. That kind of thing."

"That sounds incredibly good," Lila said crisply. "Just like old times. Let's just do the kind of normal stuff I used to do before my life got complicated." She turned to Jessica, her face softening. "But I need to stay here tonight. Please, Jessica. I can't be alone right now. I'm too afraid. I'm even afraid to go to sleep."

"Sure," Jessica agreed. Actually she was more than happy to have Lila stay. Things had been totally boring since Elizabeth had left, with no sister to harass without mercy. Plus Lila was her favorite friend. Not only was she a real-life widow of an Italian count, she was a totally fun person with tons of money of her own. And you never knew what could happen. Maybe Lila had another count hidden under her sleeve—for her!

"I don't even want to go back to my apartment," Lila said firmly.

"You can borrow my stuff," Jessica agreed instantly. "And Elizabeth's too."

"Oooh. I can't wait."

"Look," Jessica said practically. "We'll go shopping today. Then tonight we'll have a good, old-fashioned sleep over—"

"Stay awake over," Lila reminded her, turning on her side and propping herself up on her elbow.

Jessica picked up the phone and pressed a button. "Yes, this is Jessica Wakefield again in Dickenson Hall at SVU? I'd like my usual tonight at eight P.M. Yes. The superlarge combo with everything. Thanks!" She set down the phone. "JoMamma's Pizza, for starters."

"I'm feeling better already," Lila announced, sitting up cross-legged and stretching her arms over her head.

Jessica looked at her thoughtfully, then handed her another bottle of nail polish. "Get normal. That's the key word for the day. Normal."

Lila slipped a file off the table next to the bed and began working earnestly on her nails as the rain began to lash against the window. "Yes. And tomorrow I'll break up with Damon for good."

Chapter
Thirteen

"Stop!" Lila wailed.

"Don't get crazy on me." Jessica laughed. "If you don't like it, it washes right out."

Lila sat helpless on Jessica's desk chair, wrapped in a bedsheet. "I don't like the idea of *mango*, Jessica."

"Mango with hot sunset highlights," Jessica reminded her, tipping the chair back so that Lila's head hovered over a large plastic bowl. "It's only temporary hair color, Lila. Now don't move."

"And I don't like feeling like an Egyptian mummy either." Lila began laughing. "This bedsheet is so tight, I can't even move my arms. I feel like you're about to embalm me and lock me into your secret little dorm tomb."

Jessica smiled as she continued massaging the orange foam into Lila's hair. "This stuff will make your hair shine forever, Lila, even after I've mummified you."

Lila burst out laughing again. "I can't believe I let you do this."

"I can't believe we ate twelve pieces of pizza," Jessica noted.

"I bet my hair is going to be the color of that pizza sauce," Lila pointed out.

"It's not!" Jessica protested, squeezing out the excess color foam and wrapping Lila's head in an old beach towel. "It will give you more auburn highlights. Dr. Damon won't recognize you!"

Lila's face dimmed. "That would be good."

Jessica waved her away. "Stop worrying about him. He sounds like a really strange guy. You made a mistake, that's all. Bruce will be back from Japan in a few months, and everything will be back to normal."

Lila nodded seriously and said nothing.

Jessica wiped off her hands and gazed sadly at Lila, though inside she wasn't really feeling sad at all. Actually, sometimes there was nothing better for the human spirit than having a friend in misery who needed a little uplifting. It was funny how comforting it could be and how it could actually make your own depressing and pitiful problems seem small in comparison. Imagine. Even rich, beautiful, classy Lila Fowler had problems! Terrible problems!

Plus Jessica had nothing better to do on a

Saturday night. Compared to hanging out with her other sorority sisters, Lila was a tornado of fun, even in her miserable state.

"While the color sets, I want you to give me another makeover," Jessica ordered Lila.

Lila rolled her eyes. "I've already made you over five times, Jessica. It's going to give you a skin rash."

Jessica tossed a wedge of her blond hair back and stared at her reflection in the big vanity mirror. "We've done supermodel, punk, minimalist, space-age, and Elizabeth-Wakefield-prom. Now I want the fifties. I want Marilyn Monroe."

"Oooh!" Lila perked up. She held on to her towel and padded over to Jessica. "I'd like to do Marilyn." She pointed to Jessica's cheek. "A cute little mole there. Lots of black eyeliner."

"Mmmm. Big red lips," Jessica agreed, making her lips pout. "I've got a skintight gold lamé dress I could wear."

"Would you sing for me when we're done?" Lila said dryly.

Jessica laughed and jabbed Lila lightly on the arm. It was past nine o'clock, and they'd been playing with clothes and makeup for hours.

"Let's call Let's Eat and have them deliver that Chinese chicken salad," Lila said thoughtfully, dabbing the end of Jessica's eyeliner with the tip of her tongue.

Jessica put her hands on her hips. "We've already had dinner."

"Eating helps me forget," Lila contradicted.

Jessica shrugged. "As long as you're paying." She checked her watch. "Hey! It's time for you to wash out that color now. Just shower it off. It won't turn your body orange. At least I don't think so."

Lila made a face and set down the eyeliner. "OK, *Marilyn*. I'll be back in a sec."

Jessica sighed as the door closed and continued applying a thick line of black above her lashes. She felt a pang. It was good to have Lila there, but it was also true that she was skipping out on a major good time that night since Lila was too paranoid to go out.

She made a face. The university was hosting a regional beach volleyball tournament that weekend, and even though the games were practically rained out, a big postgame outdoor dance was under way under tents in the quad. In fact, the dance had pretty much drained everyone from Dickenson Hall. The usually noisy halls were quiet, the eerie silence broken only occasionally by the flush of a distant toilet, the ding of an elevator, or the wind as it whistled against the building.

Jessica painted her lids, then reached for her mascara wand. Though the rain had temporarily died down, the wind had picked up, clattering the half open miniblind against the frame of her window. She looked back sharply over her shoulder, then back toward the mirror.

"And now for a little blush," Jessica murmured to

herself, snapping open one of her sister's compacts. She smoothed a hint of color across her cheek, then softened it with her fingertip.

She hummed as she reached again for her dark pencil to create the Marilyn Monroe mole. But a soft squeaking sound made her suddenly stop.

Jessica turned around slowly and frowned. The room, now heaped with discarded clothes, hairstyling equipment, and cosmetics, stood silent and undisturbed. But there was something different in the air now—a strange feeling that someone was nearby.

The miniblind jangled again, and Jessica jumped. She lifted her head and stared at the window, her heart suddenly beating in her rib cage like the wings of a bird. The blind was half open, but her room was on the second floor, so no one could see inside unless she was standing directly in front of the window.

"What is wrong with me?" Jessica muttered, shaking off her feelings and turning back to the mirror. She picked out a deep red lipstick and began applying it carefully to her mouth.

Actually Jessica knew what was wrong. She was *not* used to playing prisoner in the university dorms on Saturday night, especially on a weekend when the campus was literally crawling with cute volleyball athletes assembled from all over the West Coast.

She let out a weary sigh, pressed her lips together, and stood back to check out the effect.

Lila's going to owe me, big *time.*

Jessica stared at her reflection, pouted her lips, and twisted her long hair on top of her head, tipping back her head and giving the mirror a sexy pose. She was just about to drop her hair back down when she thought she saw something flutter briefly in the corner of her eye. Something in the reflection. Something behind her.

Dropping her arms, Jessica whirled around and faced the window again. The blind jiggled, and blowing rain tapped against the glass. Outside she could hear the distant sound of thumping dance music in the quad and the wail of the wind and rain in the trees. She stood perfectly still. There was another sound too. Stealthy. Unnatural. She'd never heard that one before.

Jessica bit her lip, gathering the courage to tiptoe to the window and look out into the darkness. Or at least close the blind all the way.

Where is Lila?

Then Jessica suddenly remembered. There *was* the fire escape ladder. Nothing very major. Just rusted-out metal rungs that ran along the side of her window on the way down from the roof and stopped seven feet or so above the ground. Hardly noticeable. Yet what if someone . . .

Jessica took another step forward.

Where is Lila?

Finally Jessica shoved down her fear and marched forward toward the window, intending

203

to shut the miniblind and stop worrying once and for all. But as she neared, there was a sharp flicker of movement and a gray outline of a shape that made her heart lurch.

"Oh no!" Jessica gasped, suddenly realizing that the outline had been a face—and that the face had been one she thought she recognized. Almost as soon as she saw it, though, it disappeared, and Jessica ran frantically to the window. She yanked hard on the miniblind cord to open it, only to discover that she had accidentally dropped it shut.

"Aagh!" Jessica cried out in frustration, yanking the blind up again, opening the window, and sticking her head out into the wind and rain just in time to see a man scramble down to the bottom rung, then jump to the ground in one swift, graceful movement.

She squinted, trying desperately to see the face again. But all she could see now was the figure of a tall, dark-haired man, hurrying away through the bushes and scuttling leaves.

Jessica stepped away from the window and drew her hands up to her face in fright, realizing that she really didn't need to see the face again because it had been unforgettable.

It had been the face of Damon Price.

She glanced at the door, now praying that Lila would not walk through at this exact moment. Not until she had a few moments to calm down.

I can't tell Lila that her creepy boyfriend is stalking

her now, she thought miserably. *What's that going to do to her state of mind? She's already totally freaked. If I told her I saw Damon Price at the window, she'd probably run away. And where would she go?*

Jessica paced back and forth, her hands clasped tightly and her knuckles white. There were two ways a crazy guy like that could get into the room. One was through the window. And one was through the dorm's front doors.

She turned, rushed toward the window, and slammed it shut, locking the latch securely. Her head was spinning. What about the front doors? They were monitored around the clock by a security guard at the front desk. All other entrances to the building were locked shut.

"Thank goodness for campus security," Jessica breathed, collapsing back on her bed. "There's no way he can get up here. This is probably the safest place she can be."

"I never felt as if I had to explain myself to Damon," Lila said softly. She was sitting cross-legged on Elizabeth's bed, reading a brand-new book from her favorite romance series.

Across the room Jessica was reading too, propped up on a big pillow, slowly turning the pages of a fashion magazine, her blond hair spread out like a halo on her pillow. *So strangely silent,* Lila thought, after all those wild and crazy things they did all day.

Lila shrugged. *She's probably exhausted.*

"When I was with him," Lila went on, "I finally understood the feeling of being two halves of a whole."

Jessica turned another page. "Mmmm."

Lila clenched her fists on top of the blanket. "I don't understand what happened to him."

"Well"—Jessica yawned—"he's no longer a half of your whole, Li. Forget him."

Lila swallowed hard. "You don't understand. It wasn't just that he was attracted to the way I looked—we saw the same things. Felt the same way. We even finished each other's sentences. So when the dreams began, it almost seemed logical. I mean, we were so connected in real life, it made sense that we would be together in my dreams—even if it was in another time."

Jessica was silent.

"Now he's completely cold," Lila said. "And I can't figure out why."

Jessica's eyelashes fluttered.

"Jessica?" Lila spoke up, looking over. "You're not falling asleep on me, are you? You promised to stay awake. If I fall asleep, I'll have another horrible nightmare. I just know it."

Lila could see Jessica's glance dart toward her digital clock. "It's almost two A.M., Lila," Jessica mumbled.

"Don't wimp out on me," Lila ordered.

"Mmmm."

"That first night we had dinner—at Andre's," Lila went on softly in the darkness, "was the most romantic night of my life."

Lila was about to launch into a detailed description of the meal and the conversation, knowing the memories would help keep her awake. But there was an abrupt noise to her right, like the sharp intake of a car engine, and Lila knew her stay-awake-overnight plans with Jessica had fallen through.

Jessica was actually snoring. Once, then twice, then a third time loudest of all.

Lila's lips pursed tightly as she stared at her friend, her mouth half open in sleep, her magazine slipped to the floor, her arm hanging out of the bed.

"Thanks, Jessica," Lila whispered, her own eyelids beginning to sag. "I can tell you really care."

Lila forced her eyes open, scared to death of falling asleep. She decided to block Damon from her mind. It was too painful to think about him. She'd fallen in love with him so quickly and intensely. It was just too hard to contemplate the fact that their union was doomed.

She searched her mind desperately for good thoughts and suddenly, unexpectedly, found herself thinking of Bruce. Her heart began to lift just thinking of his handsome face and the wild and fun times they always had together.

Yes, Bruce is probably the one for me, Lila thought with determination, hoping she could surf on the energy of Bruce Patman memories and stay awake for just . . . a . . . few . . . more . . . hours. . . .

Flora was struggling to pull herself up off the kitchen floor, but the pounding pain in the side of her body was overwhelming. She lay back, exhausted, her blue dressing gown sprawled about, her chest tight with fear.

She raised her chin slightly, trying to look around the room. What was happening? Through her foggy daze she had only the vaguest memory of someone picking her up and flinging her against the wall. . . .

Theodore?

Had it been her own husband? The man she adored?

"No," Flora moaned. "Not my Theo. Please, not Theo."

Flora drew her knees up to her chest and tried to roll over onto her side. She had to get up. She had to find a way back to her room. To Theodore.

"Where do you think you're going?" A loud voice stabbed into her thoughts, echoing in the metal kitchen.

Stunned, Flora rolled back on the bare floor so that she was looking up at the ceiling again. Theodore was there now, his face ashen and glistening with sweat. His eyes, darker than two lumps of coal, stared down at her.

"Theo, please . . . ," Flora begged.

Theodore lowered his face so that it was inches from hers. His face, smooth only moments ago, now shadowed with dark stubble; his lips were cracked and raw. "Shut up!" he shouted.

Flora gasped, trying desperately to inch herself away on her elbows. "Theo, no . . ."

"You took it all! You're a thief. The paintings were mine!" he screamed, reaching his two hands down toward her neck.

Flora dug her heels into the floor. She tried to slide back away from him and roll to her feet, but Theodore's hands caught her throat.

Rough hands, Flora thought, though at the same time she realized the thought was odd. So odd. Theodore always kept his hands so soft. So beautifully manicured. So strong. *Yes, so strong,* her mind told her as the hands locked around her neck and began to squeeze.

Flora could feel the pressure of blood filling her head, squeezing out her temples and cheeks. Her chest clenched with pain. Her eyes were bulging from the pressure, and she found that she couldn't close them, even to shut out the sight of the man who was ending her life. The man who didn't move his head or even blink as he stared down at her, squeezing tighter and tighter. . . .

*   *   *

"Aaaaagh!" Lila screamed, reaching up to her throat, desperately trying to peel away the powerful fingers that were throttling her. Finally, with a burst of superhuman effort, she ripped them away and felt the air rushing back painfully into her nearly crushed windpipe.

She gasped and gasped again for breath.

"Damon!" she finally managed to cry out. "Damon, why are you doing this? Why are you trying . . . to kill me?"

She felt his presence near, though her eyes were still closed. His breath was like a wintry draft on her cheek, and she waved it away with her hands. "Go away! Go away, Damon. Stop!"

In the distance she could hear a voice. A softer voice. It was calling her back gently, overtaking Damon's dark presence. Soothing her and . . .

"Lila," the voice was calling. Her shoulders were being shaken. "Lila, wake up! You're OK. It's just a dream."

Lila swallowed and stirred. She opened her eyes and looked out at the grainy light in the room. She felt the smoothness of sheets surrounding her body. The solid walls. The dorm bed across from hers. Then Jessica's face hovering over her like a beacon.

"Lila?" Jessica said.

Lila frowned and reached up to rub her eyes. There was a tingling sensation in her neck but silence,

210

darkness, peace. "I—I had a—horrible dream."

"Yeah. I guess *so*," Jessica said. "You were waving your hands in the air and screaming. It took me forever to wake you up."

Lila groaned and turned over, tears filling her eyes. "It was so real, Jessica. So real."

Jessica was rubbing her back. "I thought you were never going to wake up."

"It was terrible . . . terrible," Lila whispered, lifting her right hand up to her throat as if to soothe it.

"What happened?"

Lila closed her eyes, a part of her wanting to forget the dream and yet another part wanting to understand it. "The nightmare doesn't end."

Jessica looked impatient. "What do you mean, it doesn't end?"

"It keeps moving forward," Lila tried to explain. "It picks up right where it left off."

Jessica's eyes darkened. "You mean something happened after the guy threw you against the wall?"

Lila's lips trembled as she nodded. "I woke up on the floor, and I was Flora again."

Jessica nodded. "Yeah. Flora who is now in a beautiful bathrobe floating down a beautiful hallway *encrusted* with expensive paintings since Theodore is now successful and rich again. Only now she is in the newly remodeled kitchen."

Lila glared at her. "Are you making fun of me?"

211

Jessica's blue-green eyes widened, and she held her palms up in protest. "No way. I'm just retelling the facts."

Lila sighed. "When the dream started again, I was on the kitchen floor and Theodore was staring down at me, only he wasn't the same Theodore I'd left sleeping peacefully in bed."

"Mmmm."

"Then he accused me of stealing his money and his ideas again," Lila went on. "And then he started strangling me."

Jessica's hand flew up to her own neck. "Yuck."

Lila looked at her seriously. "The newspaper article said that Flora Grey died of wounds around the neck and that her husband was a suspect in her murder. Don't you see? It's all happening in my dream, just the way it happened in real life."

Jessica looked skeptical. "The article said crazy Theodore was a suspect?"

Lila nodded.

Jessica shrugged. "That doesn't mean he did it. I mean, wasn't there a trial or an investigation or something?"

Lila stared. "I don't know."

Jessica put her hands on her hips. "Well, why don't you know?"

"Because I didn't do enough research, I guess," Lila said thoughtfully. "It was probably a big news story back then. You're right—if I keep searching for stories, I might find out the truth about who killed Flora Grey. Maybe it was Theodore—"

"And maybe it wasn't," Jessica finished, her eyes gleaming.

"Then you'll come with me to the library?"

Jessica looked shocked. "Who? Me?"

Lila nodded. "I need to figure this out, Jessica. And you've got to help me."

Chapter Fourteen

"Come on, Jessica!" Lila yelled over her shoulder. She was walking briskly ahead on the path that led from Dickenson Hall across the green to a group of academic buildings in the distance.

Jessica shivered and pulled up the zipper on her white sweater. The windy storm had been followed by a downpour all night. Then a coastal fog had moved in, once again enshrouding Sweet Valley University. Everything looked spooky and drippy in the filmy morning light.

"I shouldn't have worn my sandals," Jessica grumbled. "The grass is totally wet and gross."

"The library is up this way." Lila pointed up to her right as she turned off onto a path that wound between two stucco buildings bordered by rows of deserted bike racks. Outdoor lights over the path flicked on and off confusedly in the dim morning light.

"It is?" Jessica wondered out loud. "I always thought it was on the other end of campus, near the science buildings."

Lila paused to wait for Jessica, rolling her eyes with exasperation. "You can't be serious."

Jessica shrugged. "Why would I be?"

"Good question," Lila replied.

Don't sound sarcastic or anything, Jessica thought as she continued trudging along behind her friend. *She's got a lot of nerve. First she keeps me away from a completely huge and important dance in the quad on a Saturday night. Then she keeps me up into the middle of the night with her stories and wakes me up with her screams. And now she's dragging me to the library at ten o'clock on a Sunday morning. The whole world is asleep except us!*

Lila kept hurrying down the path, her disheveled hair flapping against the back of her sweatshirt.

Jessica could feel her hair drooping from the beads of fog in the air. "Wait up, Lila!"

Lila finally slowed down, and they walked together up the stairs of a large building Jessica vaguely recognized. "OK. This is it. It's supposed to open at ten o'clock, and if we're lucky, the microfiche room will be open."

Jessica stared. "The *what* room?"

Lila sighed and pushed open the big front door to the university library. Once inside, Jessica looked around the entrance hall and wrinkled her nose.

The place was deserted except for a middle-aged woman reading a book at a massive circular counter and a student pushing a huge cart of books into a forest of bookshelves. There was a strong smell of ink and dust, and Jessica was overcome with a sudden longing to walk back out the door.

"What do we do now?" Jessica whispered, only half joking. "Check in? Show ID? Prove that our grade point average is above two-point-oh?"

Lila rolled her eyes as they headed up a wide flight of stairs. "Jessica. You promised you would help me."

"I know. I will. Just give me a minute to adjust," Jessica said, gritting her teeth.

"Here we are," Lila said finally, opening a glass door to a separate room filled with computers and other equipment. She sat down in front of the nearest computer and pulled a chair over for Jessica. "I'm going to do a computer search of all the articles in *The New York Times* published in the month after Flora's death."

Jessica sat down next to Lila, her eyes drooping. She propped up her chin with her elbow, trying to stay awake. "Where in the *world* did you learn to do this?"

Lila typed at the keyboard, her haggard face reflecting the blue-gray of the computer screen. "Here. At the library." Several lines of information popped up after a few moments, and Lila dug into her purse excitedly for paper and pencil. "I've got some more dates."

Jessica's eyes popped open. "Dates?"

Lila glared at her. "Not that kind of date, Jessica. Come on!"

Jessica closed her eyes again.

Lila scribbled furiously. "It looks like there were at least three articles written about Flora's death after her obituary on September 14, 1937."

"Great." Jessica tried to sound enthusiastic.

"OK," Lila said nervously, standing up and looking around. "Now if I can just remember how to . . ."

Jessica stared as Lila studied a series of file cabinet drawers, opened one, then began flipping back through a series of envelopes. Finally she pulled one out. "September–October 1937."

After drawing out a squarish-looking film negative, Lila dropped it on the floor, then retrieved it and tried to stick it in several different ways into the machine.

"May I help you girls?" a stern voice interrupted.

Jessica stood up. "Um—are you going to kick us out or something? We're not supposed to be here, are we?"

The woman pursed her lips irritably, took the microfiche from Lila's hand, and slipped it correctly into the machine. "You are welcome to use the library if you are SVU students."

"Oh," Jessica said, disappointed.

Lila began searching through the microfiche, turning the knob at the side of the machine back and forth until she finally stopped and her eyes widened with interest.

"What?" Jessica whispered.

Lila covered her eyes. "I'm afraid to read this."

Jessica dropped her head back down into her folded arms. "Are you kidding?"

"I'm serious, Jessica," Lila murmured.

"Read it," Jessica ordered. She sat up in her seat and drew up her knees, trying to stay awake. "We came all the way over here when we were supposed to be getting our beauty sleep."

"OK," Lila murmured, looking back at the screen. She bit her lip and began to read. *"Grey Autopsy Report Offers No New Evidence."*

Lila and Jessica exchanged glances.

"The Flora Grey murder investigation received a stunning blow this morning," Lila continued, *"when Long Island County coroner Dr. James Wilcox announced that Mrs. Grey's death had been caused by cardiac arrest."*

Lila gasped. "You read, Jessica. I can't."

Jessica moved forward and squinted into the screen. *"Mrs. Grey's husband, celebrated painter Theodore Grey, had been arrested shortly after her death when it appeared that the twenty-five-year-old Mrs. Grey had suffered numerous wounds about the neck following an argument overheard by several neighbors and household staff members.*

"Though some bruising was found on Mrs.

218

Grey's neck,' said Dr. Wilcox, 'death was not found to be by asphyxiation but by the sudden and spontaneous seizure of the heart.'

"Contrary to earlier police reports, Mrs. Grey was not found to have stab wounds on the neck or body, prompting Long Island County authorities to drop charges against Mr. Grey, who was released and cleared of all suspicion shortly after the coroner's announcement.

"Mr. Grey, who had steadfastly denied any wrongdoing, told reporters that his wife's death was a 'personal tragedy he was still unable to comprehend or cope with.' In later remarks he called his wife 'the light of my life and my reason for living. She was the inspiration for all the work that was important to me.'"

"What else?" Lila murmured in a low, scared voice. "Does it say anything else?"

"Nope," Jessica said. "That's it."

Lila stood up abruptly from her library chair and clasped her fingers around her neck. Her body suddenly went cold, and a dizzy feeling that had started in her head began to sink into her stomach. Tears welled up in her eyes.

"Lila, you're white," Jessica warned her. "Sit down or you'll faint."

Lila just stood there, gripping her neck more tightly, as if it would help her remember the dream.

"Lila?"

"He killed her, Jessica," Lila sobbed. "The

newspapers were wrong. I know he killed her."

She felt Jessica's arm slipping around her waist. "Calm down."

But Lila stood stock-still, paralyzed in the middle of the microfiche room, her hands still locked around her own neck, her eyes shut tightly. "I was there. It was all in the dream. He had me on the floor, and his eyes . . . his eyes were on fire. He put his hands around my neck and was squeezing so hard, Jessica. So hard."

"Lila! Snap out of it!" Jessica insisted. "Or I'll call that nasty old librarian."

"But I saw it happening," Lila went on, barely hearing her friend. "I know the truth."

Jessica shook her gently. "So? What difference does it make anymore? It happened ages ago!"

"You still don't understand?" Lila cried, opening her eyes wide and staring at Jessica. "It's happening all over again! Only it's not Theodore and Flora. It's me and Damon."

Jessica opened her mouth, closed it again, and sat down.

"Don't you see?" Lila said, dropping down on her knees next to Jessica. "Theodore and Flora were madly in love until another personality seemed to take Theodore over, destroying his work, their marriage, and eventually Flora's life."

"Yes, but—"

"It's the same thing with me and Damon," Lila

insisted. "It's as if the past were pulling us back. Damon was always obsessed by the woman's face in the Theodore Grey paintings. My face. And now I'm obsessed by these strange dreams. Damon's face."

Jessica looked uncertain.

Lila wrung her hands in grief. "Look at the similarities, Jessica. Now Damon is changing right before my eyes, just like Theodore did. There's a crazy, unpredictable, cold side to him, and I know it's not because I'm going crazy. Damon is going to kill me, just like Theodore killed Flora."

Jessica was beginning to look frightened.

"I know it sounds crazy," Lila went on, "but I keep thinking that there were injuries from the past—really bad injuries—that somehow need to be relived."

Jessica was quiet for a long moment before she finally spoke, her blue-green eyes gleaming. "Maybe we should check it out."

"What do you mean, check it out?" Lila wanted to know. "Who would you possibly check it out with?"

"You know," Jessica said matter-of-factly, "one of those experts on past life stuff."

"What?"

Jessica shrugged. "Reincarnation and all that."

Lila looked at her in disbelief. "How would you know about that, Jessica?"

"From the movies," Jessica replied. "They explain everything."

*　　　*　　　*

221

Flora felt the grass so cool beneath her feet. The scent of white roses filled the air, and the sun fell in dapples through the leaves of a spreading walnut tree.

"Keep your lovely chin up for one more moment, my darling," Theodore murmured from behind his easel. He leaned his head out and studied her face as he worked his paintbrush over the canvas.

Flora felt bubbles of laughter inside. Theodore looked so terribly funny squinting at her that way. "What is that, Theo? Oh, look. A dab of paint at the tip of your nose."

"Stop it, Flora," Theodore warned, trying to be stern. "You mustn't."

Flora suddenly threw back her head with laughter. "Oh, I'm so sorry, dear. You make me so happy, I can't seem to . . .

She felt his lips on hers suddenly, so warm and full of passion. . . .

"I love you, my dear, darling wife. . . ."

"I love you too, Theo," Flora said. "For always. With all my heart."

Flora felt herself fading out of consciousness, so that the bright sunlight dimmed and her lips could no longer feel the pressure of her husband's. She seemed to be floating in a black space, though ahead of her in the darkness she could see several bright, square objects moving toward her. She squinted and realized that the images were paintings. Paintings of herself, though the paintings that had once been so lovely were now brutally slashed and cut. She felt her mouth opening in a huge, silent scream. The slashes along her white painted neck, pouring red blood . . .

Now even the paintings were gone, and as complete and utter darkness began to descend upon her she felt a hand on each side of her neck. She struggled to shake off the hands, but as she did she found that their touch had begun to turn into a grasp and that the grasp was quickly turning into a choking hold on her throat. The hands squeezed tighter and tighter until Flora's head began to spin and her whole world began to fade away into a shadowy dream. . . .

Flora was still floating in a dark space, only she gradually became aware that her name was Lila and that someone was calling her name from a great distance.

"Lila?" a gentle voice broke through. "Lila? Are you with us now?"

Lila lifted her lids and found that she was staring into a pair of immense blue eyes framed by flowing black hair and door-knocker-size silver earrings. "Yes, I'm back," she murmured. Her arms felt so light, as if they were floating up off the arms of the chair.

"Are you OK?" she heard Jessica's scared voice to her right.

"Yes, I'm fine," Lila answered, looking about the room. She remembered coming here now with Jessica. The woman with the blue eyes was Astra Larsson, a reincarnation therapist whose yellow pages ad had read Past Life Healing—Spiritual Repair—Psychic Truth. When Jessica called her on the telephone from the library, the woman had agreed to see them in an hour and gave them directions to her office on the coast highway.

They'd driven through swirling fog to reach Ms. Larsson's office, which was a beach-front cottage converted into an office space. The front reception area faced the road, and the room where Ms. Larsson conducted her hypnotic therapy sessions opened up to the ocean, which was gray and churning in the damp air. Wind chimes clanged spookily in the wind gusts. Outside, her collection of exotic wooden statues stood silent and steadfast in the dripping damp weather.

Now Lila sat across a beautiful wooden table from Astra, who had slipped her hand into hers. The darkened room was completely upholstered in exotic silks, which reflected the shimmering lights of the dozens of flickering candles arranged on the tables and shelves surrounding them. There was the crashing sound of the nearby ocean waves, and next to Astra sat a slender dog with large ears, which she gently stroked.

"What happened?" Lila finally asked, blinking slowly.

Astra laid her hands flat on the table in front of her and smiled very gently. Her blue eyes shone brightly in her tanned face. "Your trance was very easily induced."

Jessica snapped her fingers and nodded. "Like *that*. You freaked me. And your Flora voice was so different!"

Astra smiled and placed one hand on Jessica's shoulder as if to signal for quiet, which Jessica, incredibly, seemed to understand.

"When I asked you to search back for a pleasant memory," Astra explained in her soothing, liquid voice, "you almost instantly began calling yourself Flora and described to me the grounds of a large estate, where you were with a man named Theodore, who you said was your husband."

"He *was* my husband," Lila said earnestly.

Astra raised her hand slightly and nodded. "You were outdoors together, and he was painting your picture. You could smell the roses. You kissed. . . ."

"Yes," Lila said absently.

"When I asked you to move forward in time and describe something that disappointed you, you took me through the horror of seeing your husband's paintings defaced and covered with blood."

"Yes," Lila whispered.

"Then it appeared that your mind jumped forward, Lila, and I'm afraid I was not able to stop you from reliving a terrible event once again," Astra explained. "It was a scene of inexpressible violence and hatred."

Lila felt tears rising. "Of death—"

"Yes, perhaps. You were being attacked."

Tears began to stream down Lila's cheeks, but it was partly because she was comforted to have someone take her seriously at last. Lila pressed her hands downward on the table in front of her. "The trance, the dreams—they were all recalling actual events."

"Yes," Astra said thoughtfully. "And the physical similarities you describe are quite remarkable."

"The photographs and paintings I've seen of Flora Grey look just like me," Lila agreed.

"And you say you've seen the photographs of the artist Theodore Grey," Astra prompted her. "And they resemble this friend of yours, Damon Price."

"Yes," Lila said. With every word more and more frightening details flashed across her mind. "I'm scared to death."

Astra sat back and stroked her dog. "I believe, based on the evidence you've brought me today, that you very well could be the reincarnation of Flora Grey."

Lila gasped. "You do? You don't think I'm completely crazy?"

A strange expression floated across Astra's face. A

gust of wind rattled the building, and outside, Lila could hear a loose shutter banging out of control.

Finally Astra spoke. "Do you believe these things are due to coincidence? That you would meet Damon and fall in love and that he would recognize you from the paintings he'd cherished for so many years? That you would see the Grey paintings in your dreams first before Damon ever showed them to you?"

Astra's sapphire eyes seemed to bore into Lila's. "Do you believe it's coincidence that you dreamed of Flora and Theodore Grey's personal life before discovering that what you dreamed actually happened?"

Lila put her hands on each side of her face and shook her head. "No. It's impossible."

Astra sat back, her earrings swinging. "Our bodies are only temporary shells for our souls, Lila. They do not die."

"Wow," Jessica breathed.

Astra smiled. "Don't we all have talents, feelings, thoughts, and passions that have nothing to do with our actual life experience?"

"Yes, but not everyone has dreams like this," Lila insisted. "Dreams that are reenactments of events that really happened sixty years before."

Astra nodded, gracefully winding her long, beaded necklace around her fingers as she spoke. "Often acute past life experiences like this can be brought on by a sharp blow to the head, which occurred when Damon accidentally dropped the book on your head on that first date you had together."

"I see," Lila whispered.

"You and Damon were instantly attracted to each other, but you might have never understood why without the slight head injury, which may have brought on the dreams."

"But I just want the dreams to go away!" Lila wailed. "I don't want to know another thing about Theo and Flora Grey."

"You must be strong!" Astra said abruptly, taking both of Lila's hands and looking deeply into her eyes. There was a second strong gust of wind, which suddenly blew out the candle burning between them. "The law of karma is mysterious, but it is just."

"What do you mean?" Lila asked in a tiny, scared voice.

"It means that those who cause suffering in one life are destined to pay in another. Justice is never escaped. Misdeeds are always avenged, even if it takes a thousand years. The development of the soul depends upon this great law."

Jessica paled. "That's a scary thought."

Lila bit her lip. "So if my husband murdered me in a past life, you're saying that won't necessarily happen all over again."

Astra smiled strangely. "If anything, my dear, the opposite will happen."

Lila froze. "The opposite? You mean *I* might . . . hurt him back?"

"You must be strong," Astra said, closing her eyes in meditation. "You must persevere through this difficult time."

"Well, that's easy for you to say," Lila cried, covering her face with her hands as a deadly chill began to pass through her like a knife.

Jessica was still gripping her seat in terror after Lila stood up and floated out of the room to pay the bill at Astra's front desk.

She felt Astra's hand pressing on hers. "What is it, Jessica?"

Jessica tried to relax. She cleared her throat. "Oh, it's just this cosmic payback stuff. It's got me a little creeped out."

"Yes," Astra said calmly, signaling for her dog to jump into her lap. She stroked his ears. "A soul can choose to advance or regress, you see."

Jessica made a worried face. "How do you know if you're advancing?"

Astra smiled. "Today you helped your friend. You came with her and supported her in a time of terrible need. It will come back to you, Jessica. The positive energy will always be reflected back on you, if not in this life, then in the next."

Jessica leaned closer. "But I'm still really worried right now. I mean, this Damon Price is a very,

very strange guy." Jessica looked over her shoulder and lowered her voice. "In fact, I happen to know that he's stalking her."

Astra knitted her eyebrows together. "You must be very careful."

"I don't want to tell her, though," Jessica explained. She bit her thumbnail and stood up. "She's upset enough as it is."

"Yes," Astra said thoughtfully, standing up with her and following her to the door. Her long blue dress swished against her legs. "That may be the correct approach. Your friend is a strong girl, but she doesn't understand how powerful she is."

Jessica nodded. "She's a total mess."

Astra clasped Jessica's hand in both of hers. "I can tell already that you are a loyal friend. Be strong for her. Help her."

"I promise," Jessica said solemnly.

"Don't let her out of your sight either," Astra added, opening the door and leading her into the waiting room, which had clouds painted on its ceiling.

"Yes, I—"

Suddenly a ragged, terrified scream sliced through the roar of the wind and the waves. A cold shiver ran through Jessica's body because she recognized the scream.

It was Lila's.

Chapter
Fifteen

_____

"Why did you run away from me like that, Lila?"
Damon asked in a smirking, singsong voice.

Lila had walked out of Astra's beach-front office after paying her bill, too confused and upset
to talk. She felt the cool air in her hair and reveled
in the deep crashing sound of the waves hitting
the sand. But just after she rounded the building
along the filmy path to the beach, Lila felt someone grab her upper arm and enclose it in a powerful grasp. She screamed in sheer terror.

Whirling her head around, she saw Damon's
pale, ragged face surrounded by blowing, dark
hair. She tried to yank her arm away, but his grip
tightened with every move she made. Her feet
scraped the sandy gravel, and the wind whipped
her hair into her eyes and mouth.

"I thought we were getting to be such good

friends, Lila," Damon said in an eerie voice. He flattened her against the wall of the building, the veins in his neck bulging above the neck of his grimy black T-shirt. "I thought you might even love me a little."

Lila gritted her teeth and tried to bang the side of the house with her shoulder, an effort she knew was futile since the roar of the wind and waves was doomed to drown out her call for help. "Let me go."

"All those long talks about art," Damon went on, twisting her arm behind her back. "All those sweet kisses . . ."

Lila felt him wrench her arm even further as he tried to swing her around to face him.

"You loved those kisses."

Damon's face now loomed in front of hers, almost unrecognizable. His skin was a milky gray, and his black beard stubble was even thicker. Dark circles shadowed his eyes, and his mouth looked red and raw, surrounding his wide, grinning teeth. Lila closed her eyes, the dream memory of his hands around her neck so very close, it was making her sick with dizziness.

"Why are you following me?" Lila sobbed, turning her head away from his ghoulish stare. "Why do you want to hurt me, Damon?"

"I don't want to hurt you," Damon said, grabbing her chin with his hand and squeezing it as he lifted it to his face. "I want to love you."

Lila jerked her head and back forth, trying to shake him off.

"Hey!" she heard Jessica call out angrily. Lila heard running footsteps on the gravel path behind her. *"Get your hands off her, creep!"*

Lila felt Damon's grip loosen as he turned toward Jessica in surprise. As Lila managed to lurch away she watched Jessica rush behind Damon, grab the calf of his leg, and yank him off his feet.

"Ummmphhh," Damon grunted as he landed hard on his side on the walkway.

"Come on!" Jessica shouted, grabbing Lila's hand and running with her to the Miata parked in front. "Let's get out of here!"

Lila slammed the car door, started the engine, and was screeching out of the parking lot even before Jessica was completely in the passenger seat.

"Go!" Jessica shouted as gravel flew. She smelled Lila's tires burn as they tore onto the highway at a sharp angle. The engine screamed as Lila accelerated, then dropped to a powerful hum when Lila finally downshifted.

Jessica's hair flew wildly in the open convertible. "I'm calling the police on your cell phone, Lila. What if he starts hassling Astra?"

Lila nodded, slipping on her sunglasses. Her hair flew straight back, and her mouth had settled into a tight line. Fresh bruises were beginning to show where Damon had grabbed her arm.

Jessica had to wait to speak to a police officer, who promised to check out the Larsson office.

"Lila!" Jessica called out, holding the phone. "Do you want to give the police a description of Damon and press charges against him? They'll meet us at the dorms!"

"No!" Lila shouted, slamming the cell phone down. "I'm not ready to do that, Jessica! Let's just get back to your room and figure out what to do. I need five seconds to think!"

"You're in a panic," Jessica protested. "Damon's a madman, and he's got to be stopped."

Lila's cheeks were wet where tears had rolled below her sunglasses. "I know. But it's just that it's so hard to believe. It's almost as if he's got two personalities. The only trouble is—I was in love with one of them."

Jessica made a face. "That guy outside Astra's didn't look anything like the guy I tangled with in the art lecture hall last week," she said in a disgusted voice. "*That* was Damon? Give me a break! This guy looked more like some kind of psychopathic monster. We should call the police again right now."

"He did look like a monster, didn't he?" Lila called out over the wind, wiping her wet face with her fingers. "That's the part I can't figure. How could he have changed so much, so quickly?"

Jessica shook her head. "That's what you said happened to Theodore in your dreams. One second he was fine. Flora's dream boat husband. The next second he's ripping up his paintings and trying to kill her. If Damon Price is a reincarnation of Theodore Grey, he hasn't exactly made much progress in the soul department, has he?"

"I want to forget the whole thing, Jessica," Lila said, taking the exit ramp into Sweet Valley. "Like it never happened."

Jessica sat back in her seat, exasperated. How could Lila forget the whole thing? The guy was stalking her. He was totally dangerous. What could she be thinking?

"Now I just want to focus on Bruce," Lila said, looking over hopefully at Jessica as the car slowed and entered the busy Sweet Valley boulevard. "I miss him, you know. After everything I've been through in the last week, it's really nice to know he's still there in my life, waiting for me."

Jessica froze. "Oh yeah."

"I think I'll call him tonight," Lila went on, turning off the main drag and heading toward the leafy avenues surrounding the campus.

"Tonight?" Jessica said worriedly. She could kick herself for sending him that awful letter about Lila and Damon. It had been a silly, impulsive move. Jessica had practically forgotten she'd sent it—and now she'd probably ruined any chances Lila might

235

have of getting over this insane fling of hers.

"I really need to hear his voice."

Jessica swallowed hard. By now Bruce had probably received her stupid note. He was probably ready to kill Lila, not talk to her.

Of course, Bruce is a complete jerk and spoiled brat who doesn't deserve Lila, Jessica thought. *But how am I going to live with messing up that relationship over that creepy little psychopath?*

Lila carefully parked her Miata in the Dickenson Hall dorm lot, turned off the ignition, and set the brake. She pulled out a tissue and blew her nose.

"Let's go upstairs and call the police," Jessica said. "I'm not leaving you alone until we get this whole mess straightened out."

Lila crumpled her tissue and turned to face her with a sigh. They locked eyes and smiled. "Thanks, Jessica," she said. "You're the best friend I have, and I mean it. You probably saved my life back there."

Jessica cringed inside. For some reason she couldn't bear the thought of Lila believing she was as wonderful as that. She had to get her horrible secret off her chest.

"Lila," Jessica said firmly as Lila started to get out of the car.

Lila's hand was still on the car door handle when she turned back to look. "What?"

Jessica bit down hard on her bottom lip. "I have a confession to make."

Lila let go of the handle and sat back, staring up at the blue sky. Her face was pale and still streaked where tears had fallen. "What is it now? Did you borrow money from me again and forget to tell me? Accidentally use my car and log an extra five hundred miles on it? Lose that gorgeous leopard print Hermès scarf I lent you last week?"

Jessica drew in her breath sharply. "No. I wrote Bruce and told him you were seeing Damon behind his back."

Lila's face flushed pink. She tore off her sunglasses and stared hard at Jessica. "You did *what?*"

Jessica just stared back, her eyes filling with tears.

"You . . . you . . . just *wrote* him and told him that?" Lila sputtered, taking the steering wheel in one hand as if she were trying to keep from falling over.

"Yes," Jessica said meekly.

"Let me get this straight," Lila said, her voice trembling with anger. "You just wrote him a letter and told him about Damon?"

"Yes. An angry, very short letter."

Lila's mouth dropped open. She covered her eyes with her hands, then lowered them and stared over at Jessica in wonder. "How did you get his address?"

Jessica felt sobs welling up. "You dropped a letter from him on the floor at Theta house, and I stole it."

"*Why*, Jessica?" Lila screamed. "*Why* did you do that?"

Jessica flicked away a tear. "I wrote it on an

impulse right after that idiot Damon Price tried to humiliate me about my class attendance."

"I can't believe it," Lila said flatly.

"I'm sorry," Jessica whispered. "I was mad when you went along with it. You didn't back me up, Lila."

"Get out," Lila snapped, turning away and gripping the steering wheel with one hand. With the other she quickly started the engine up again.

"But Lila, I'm worried—"

"Get out, Jessica."

Jessica slunk out of the car and shut the door.

Lila gunned the engine. "If you cared about me so much," she yelled over the roar of the car, "why did you steal my mail and send that awful letter to Bruce? Now I have no one to turn to. No one!"

"Lila!" Jessica yelled as Lila backed up at full speed, leaving a streak of rubber on the pavement before roaring off down the campus avenue, her chestnut hair blowing in the wind.

"Stop!" Jessica shouted, waving her hands over her head, then looking about desperately for her Jeep. She couldn't let Lila go off by herself now!

Where did I park that Jeep? Jessica thought wildly, running around the parking lot. *I've got to get to her apartment before it's too late! Damon is probably waiting for her there right now!*

Thump-*thump*. Thump-*thump*. Thump-*thump*.
Lila put her hand to her chest as she sped down

the street toward her apartment. Her heart had been beating wildly like that for days, it seemed.

Dam-*on*. Dam-*on*. Dam-*on*.

Her chest tightened. She knew she had to be strong, but it seemed as if everywhere she turned, there were dark forces trying to pull her down. First Damon. Then her dreams. Now even her best friend, Jessica.

"Those who cause suffering in one life are destined to pay in another life, Lila. Justice is never escaped. Misdeeds are always avenged. . . ."

"What have I done?" Lila whispered. "What have I done to deserve this?"

She slowed down, gripping the steering wheel tightly as she neared her apartment, keeping her eyes peeled for Damon's Volkswagen. As she approached her parking garage, light was beginning to fall and her headlights flickered on the line of familiar cars.

Lila steered into her parking space, hopped out, and dug for her apartment keys. It was true that Damon knew she lived there. But it was her place, and she needed to be alone. There was no Jessica here. If anything happened, she had plenty of neighbors.

Lila exhaled quickly as she entered her apartment and took in her familiar surroundings. She flicked on the lights and made sure the windows and doors were locked. Then she shut all the curtains and miniblinds and put some hot water on to boil.

It wasn't until she turned the dial on her stove

239

that she realized her hands were shaking. And then there was that tight, scary pressure in her chest, as if an elephant had stepped on it.

Lila headed down the hallway to her bedroom, then paused for the barest moment when she saw the flashing red light on her answering machine.

Be careful, she told herself. *Maybe you should just ignore the messages. Turn on the TV. Forget about everything.*

Lila sucked in her breath and marched forward. If there was anything she needed right now, it was the truth. She needed the truth from Damon. From Jessica. From Bruce. Whatever was going to happen, she was going to have to face it.

And she was probably going to have to face it alone.

She sat on the edge of her bed and punched the message button on the machine, wincing when she heard the first voice on it.

"Hi, Lila," Bruce's weary voice began. *"Um. It's me. Look. I got a note from Jessica today in the mail that said something about you and a TA. . . ."*

Lila buried her face in her hands. "Oh, Bruce. I'm so sorry—"

"Listen, Lila. I know Jessica's got an incredibly hot head, and from the look of this angry scrawl here, I can tell she's mad about something. I don't know. I guess I'm saying that I don't really know if

240

you're seeing someone else because I don't trust Jessica, OK?"

Lila's eyes grew hot with shame. She lay back on her bed and let the tears trickle out the corners of her eyes.

"If you are . . . involved . . . with someone else, though," Bruce went on, his voice even and sure, *"I want you to know that I'm still here for you and that I love you."*

Lila cried softly into her pillow.

"Please call me right away. I'll talk to you soon, then. Good night."

"Good night, Bruce," Lila whispered tearfully, vowing to never even look at another guy in her life. What more could she want than Bruce Patman? Handsome, loving, wealthy, forgiving Bruce Patman with the shiny dark hair she loved to run her fingers through and that cute little cleft in his chin. . . .

"Liiilllaaa."

Lila gasped and sat up in bed. The second message on the machine!

"Where are you, Liiila?" the singsong voice warbled in her ears. *"I need you."*

There was a long, terrifying pause on the message machine, and Lila could hear the caller breathing heavily. *"OK, then,"* the caller warned in a sweet voice. *"If you won't pick up the phone and talk to me, then I'll just have to come and fiiind you."*

There was a beep and a click as the message ended.

"No!" Lila cried, pounding the message machine with her fist. "Stop it. Stop torturing me!"

Tears were pouring from her eyes now, but Lila wiped them away and frantically grabbed for the caller ID machine, which she took in her fist and stared at.

"Five-five-five," she whispered, "five-six-two-eight."

Sobbing, Lila punched out the number on her phone and brought the receiver up to her ear. If Damon was really the one making the calls and if he was making them from his home phone, then this would be her first clue.

"Hello. This is the home of Damon Price. . . ."

Lila groaned in fear and crumpled to the floor. Though she was still holding on to the phone, she was barely aware of her surroundings. The room spun and dipped.

"It's true, then," she cried into the phone. "It *was* you," she said in a louder voice. "Everything was a lie, Damon! Everything was just a big, sick joke! All you wanted was to pretend I was Flora, didn't you, Damon? So you could get back at me the way Theodore got back at her."

Lila broke down sobbing, then gathered her wits and took a huge, steadying breath. "I want to tell you something, Damon. The police are already on to you," she lied. "They know you've been calling me and following me and torturing me. And they're on their way right now!"

242

Lila slammed down the phone, caught her breath, then began frantically punching 911 when she heard a banging on the other side of her bedroom window.

"What?" Lila cried just as she heard an even louder thudding sound behind the blinds.

"Stop!" she screamed, getting up from the floor and crawling backward on the bed.

There was the sound of splintering wood, then the crash of glass. A blast of cold air rushed in. Lila watched in horror as the entire miniblind was shoved forward into the room, ripped off its hardware and flung to the side by two bulging, badly cut forearms.

"Damon!" Lila yelled.

He was standing right in front of her now, panting heavily and staring at her with smoldering eyes that peered out from behind sweaty clumps of dark hair. Splinters of glass covered his hair and shoulders, and blood was trickling from a large gash on his cheek, but he seemed unaware of it.

"Get out of here!" Lila shouted, scrambling backward across the bed, intending to make a mad dash for the hallway. She jumped awkwardly off the bed and she tripped, and sprawled to the floor.

"Where are you going, Flora?" Damon asked quietly.

Lila looked up at him. He was grinning, his red lips cruelly stretched over his teeth. "What do you want?" she screamed, hoping someone would hear.

243

"Flooorrraaaa," he sang softly, not taking his eyes off her. "It's Theeeooodore."

"Stop!" Lila shouted, lunging for the phone on the bed.

Lila knew it was futile even before she felt his powerful hands on her shoulders, ripping her off the bed and tossing her carelessly against the wall. She felt the smash of shoulder, the searing pain of her skull cracking against the bed leg.

Thump-*thump*. Thump-*thump*. Thump-*thump*.

Lila's eyelids fluttered open. The room swooped and dipped. "We . . . could . . . have had . . . so much," she whispered, no longer aware of whether she was Flora or Lila.

His grinning face dropped down in front of hers on the floor, and she saw that he was holding the phone in his hands.

"Look, Flora," he said with a menacing laugh. He ripped the phone out of the wall, then threw it back, smashing it to pieces. "Now we won't be disturbed, will we?"

Lila let out a long, desperate cry, but she soon felt the heel of his boot thud against her head, and everything went dark.

Chapter Sixteen

Thump-*thump*. Thump-*thump*. Thump-*thump*.

There was a loud scraping sound, like the clang of metal on metal, and then laughter.

Flora struggled to open her eyes, but the pressure on her neck made it almost impossible, and the pounding of her heart seemed to drown every thought.

"Theo . . . ," she croaked, barely a whisper. Why didn't he stop squeezing her neck so? The kitchen floor was so very hard. . . .

"Flora?" she heard him calling from a great distance. "Look at this. See what I have."

Her eyelids, fluttering like moth wings, looked briefly out at a world that seemed to be fading away into grays and deeper grays. There was a glint of metal, and her body jerked in desperation against the ever tightening hand.

It's a knife, she realized with a sudden rejuvenating wave of panic. *A knife. A knife.*

Thump-*thump.* Thump-*thump.* Thump-*thump.*

Flora watched his powerful arm as it slowly rose above her head, the knife shimmering above it. Yet the fear of the knifepoint seemed to fade as the pounding in her chest grew more ferocious. There was a sharp explosion of pain that began to radiate into the center of her being.

This is how I die, Flora thought. *This is the moment when I am no longer. I can feel it.*

With one final burst of strength Flora opened her eyes to look into Theo's. She saw his face, dark and wild, bearing down like a demon over her. She saw the shining knife blade descending slowly so that it was now only inches from the skin of her throat.

Thump-*thump.* Thump-*thump.* Thump-*thump.*

"Flora!" she heard him cry out, though as she glimpsed him his lips did not move.

"What are you doing?" he screamed. "What are you doing to my wife? How could you do this?"

There was a sudden release of pressure from her neck and a rush of air, though the squeezing pain inside her chest had worsened and her struggle for air was just as desperate. Above, the grimacing face of her husband had pulled back, and in its place were two faces struggling against each other.

"No," Flora gasped with the last of her air.

Two Theodores now, she thought. *Two Theodores. Fighting. Why?*

Flora felt a final bursting sensation in her chest. Her mind blurred in dark confusion. The pain lifted as she slipped into shadow. *Such a black, black place,* she thought with sudden calm, just as a flash of blinding, blissful light lifted her from the place where she lay and sent her upward into indescribable brilliance.

It was nearly dark by the time Jessica finally found her Jeep, parked illegally in a spot reserved for the dorm kitchen staff. After taking precious seconds to rip off some of the angry letters and campus parking tickets Scotch taped and soaked to the windshield, she leaped in the driver's seat, started the engine, and screeched out of the lot.

"I'm coming, Lila," Jessica sobbed, forgetting to stop before pulling onto the campus street, nearly crashing into two students on bikes.

She gunned the engine and tore down the dark street toward Lila's apartment, which was an interminable six blocks away, barely able to see through her tears and the remaining papers and tape flapping crazily from the windshield.

"I'm so sorry, Lila," Jessica cried, cursing herself for picking that moment to tell Lila about her stupid letter to Bruce. "I'm a stupid, ungrateful, foolish friend."

By the time she neared the front entrance to Lila's apartment, she was praying she could get inside. The private parking garage in back was always locked and only accessible by a remote control device. But the front entrance to the courtyard was often unlocked.

When she turned the corner, however, her hands clutched the steering wheel so hard, her knuckles turned white. A yellow Volkswagen had just pulled up in front of the courtyard gate.

Jessica gasped. The driver of the car was in such a hurry that the left wheels had jumped the curb and had plowed up a long strip of brown earth in the sidewalk grass.

"It's him!" she gasped. Lila had told her about Damon's car. A Volkswagen. She jammed on the brakes and stopped the Jeep just in back of the Volkswagen. Then she leaped out onto the sidewalk and ran up behind the dark-haired guy who'd just jumped out of the car and was running toward the gate to Lila's courtyard.

"Lila!" the guy was shouting as he ran ahead.

"Stop!" Jessica shrieked, running up from behind him. In one desperate leap she jumped on his back, threw her elbow around his neck, and with all her strength began trying to yank him to the ground. "Stay away from her, Damon!"

"What?" he croaked.

Jessica jammed her knees into the sides of his

248

muscular back and tightened her arm around his neck. "Get away from her!"

Damon had brought his hands to his throat and was trying to pry Jessica off. "Get . . . away. Who are you?"

Jessica tussled mightily, trying to shake him off his feet. "It doesn't matter," she screamed. "Just get away from my friend, Damon!"

Jessica felt his body jerk to one side and she was flung off his back into the grass, though she still managed to hang on to his forearm. She looked up as he moved toward the gate. She narrowed her eyes and studied him.

Even in the dark she could tell it was the same guy. Definitely the same dark-haired, green-eyed, cute-looking creep who'd humiliated her in his lecture hall, then attacked Lila at Astra's beach house.

A car passed, and a pair of headlights slid across his body. Sure, he'd somehow managed to change his shirt and make himself look a little more presentable on his way back from the beach.

But it was him all the same.

Jessica scrambled to her feet, ran ahead of Damon, and plastered herself in front of the gate to Lila's courtyard.

"Lila," he called out through cupped hands. "It's me, Damon. Let me in!"

"What do you think you're doing?" Jessica panted, securing her arms across the gate.

"I'm Damon Price," he said, his eyes wild and fearful. "What's wrong with you? I'm trying to get into Lila's place. She's—"

"I know all about what you want," Jessica snapped. She could feel the slivers from Lila's wooden gate stinging in her elbows, but she didn't move a muscle. "You've been harassing her and following her all weekend, and if you take another step forward, I'm going to scream!"

Damon was shaking his head. "No, you don't underst—"

"The police come *very quickly* in this neighborhood when young ladies scream, for your information," Jessica shouted at him, praying he wouldn't attack her like he'd attacked Lila.

Damon tried to reach around her body for the handle to the gate, but she yanked his hand away. "Not on your life!" she screamed.

"You don't understand," Damon said earnestly. "That wasn't me."

"Oh, right," Jessica snarled back. "Then how come you seem to know all about it? Huh? How can you deny that I saw you practically killing my best friend at Astra's place less than an hour ago?"

Damon's face contorted with pain. She could see tears flooding his eyes. "Please. Please let me open the gate. If Lila's your friend, you're going to have to trust me—"

"Over my dead body!" Jessica shouted into his

face, pushing her back even more tightly into the gate and staring into his eyes with the meanest, most threatening gaze she'd ever given anyone in her life.

At first Lila saw only grainy light through half opened lids. She knew she was awake, but the light was dim, and her first thought was that she had been killed. A stabbing terror drove through her. If she completely opened her eyes, would she discover that she was dead?

Then she realized that she could move a little and that the effort sent a sharp pain through her body. It was almost a relief since she was pretty sure that dead people felt no pain. Slowly she began to sense that she was sitting on a hard surface, her arms bound tightly behind her back, her ankles tied together in front of her.

She opened her mouth to speak, but a stocking had been stretched across her jaw and tied behind her head, gagging her.

"Uuuhhhggg," she groaned, struggling to move.

"Oh," his voice gradually broke the silence, "hello there, Flora. What a beautiful, beautiful apartment you have. I've been looking at it. You have such a comfortable couch. Soft carpets. Lovely lotions and soaps in your bathroom that smell just like you. . . ."

Lila sucked in her breath as Damon's cut and bloodied face suddenly popped in front of her, grinning horribly. Her eyes darted to the right, where his fist held a glinting knife, pointed at her neck.

She jerked her head back instinctively, only to wince in pain. The back of her neck had been jabbed with something razor sharp.

"I wouldn't do that if I were you, Flora." The grinning face mocked her. "You see, Flora, I don't just have *this* knife." He jerked forward and stuck the edge of the blade against her throat.

Lila tried to scream through the gag, but it came out muffled and low.

"I have another knife too," he said in a taunting voice. He drew his face into a serious pose. "See? Well, I guess you can't see, Flora. Because it's right behind your neck here."

Lila moaned in agony.

"I thought," Damon said in an eerie, matter-of-fact voice, "that if I wedged my *other* knife between the dishwasher and the cabinet, then I could use both at once. Neat, huh?"

Lila felt faint.

"Sooooooo," Damon continued, pointing toward the knife in his hand. "You move forward—whoops! You move backward—bingo!"

Lila was trying desperately not to fall over. She held herself perfectly still, her eyes darting about the room, looking for something—*anything*—she could do to distract him or get the attention of someone near.

"Escape is not possible, Flora," Damon said softly into her ear. She could feel his wet breath on her neck. He settled himself closer to her, his cut and bloodied face only inches from hers. "I've worked it all out. Did you know that I'm really a very smart person? My whole life everyone told me that."

Lila's arms ached. She was dizzy from lack of air.

"So this is what I've always asked myself, Flora," Damon went on. "Why didn't *I* get to go to the best schools? Why didn't *I* travel all over the world, looking at beautiful things and studying books?"

Lila stared at him. She stared at the little scar over his eyebrow. What was wrong with him? Damon *had* done all of those things.

"And *why*," he continued, his voice rising dangerously, "didn't I ever have a very rich"—he flicked her chin with his knife—"very beautiful woman like you for my very, very own?"

There was a long silence, and Lila watched in horror as the knife in Damon's hand began to tremble. His knuckles were white with tension, and beads of sweat and blood were trickling down the side of his face in tiny streams. His eyes seemed to roam her face for an answer. Sad, lonely, terrified eyes. Eyes she was sure deep down in her heart she'd never looked inside before.

She watched as his face began to crumple. Sobs convulsed his body, bringing the knifepoint closer and closer to her neck as if he didn't even realize it.

It was clear that he was lost in a faraway memory and that the memory had disturbed him deeply.

"Damon," he suddenly whispered.

Lila's eyes widened.

"Damon had all of those things. Mom . . . Dad sent him to the Academy. They sent me home!"

Lila was suddenly overcome with confusion. What was he talking about? Why was he talking about Damon as if he were another person?

"Damon," he said, gripping his knife tighter and looking at its shaking tip, "went to Harvard, you know. Then he traveled aaall over the world studying his precious *art*."

Lila's head was swimming now. What was happening? She shut her eyes tightly, making herself remember the dream. Yes, the dream. There were two Theodores in her dream. Two Theodores fighting over her as one held the knife. . . .

Twins, Lila suddenly thought as her chest tightened, tightened, tightened. It was the only explanation. Damon. The *real* Damon really *had* left town.

Or had she completely lost it?

"Damon thought he could keep me locked away in that place," the man cried out. He sat back cross-legged on the floor, rocking back and forth, staring at the knife in his hand. "He's ashamed of me. He wanted me out of his sight!"

Lila tried to breathe deeply. She was sucking for air now, and the pressure in her chest seemed to mount with each passing moment.

"Well, Damon was wrong," the guy screamed, still rocking back and forth. "Because I broke out of that terrible place, and I came back to take away what he's taken from me!"

The man reached over and loosened the stocking gag in her mouth. Then he slowly pulled it down and caressed her lower lip with his bloody thumb. "It's too bad, really, because you are so very, very lovely, Flora."

"My name is Lila," Lila whispered hoarsely.

The guy threw back his head and began to laugh hysterically. Blood poured from a gash on his temple. Lila tried to struggle against the rope around her wrists, but the knifepoint at her neck cut into her flesh whenever she moved.

"I know all the cute little pet names you and Damon have for each other," he sneered. "Theodore. Flora. It's sick, Lila. Sick. Sick."

Lila swooned. Outside the kitchen window she heard a commotion. People were arguing. Jessica?

"Now," the man said, gripping the knife and holding it in front of her face. "Give me a kiss, Lila. Give me a good-bye kiss. For Damon. I'll tell him you said good-bye."

Lila sucked in a huge gulp of air and let out the loudest, most bloodcurdling scream of her life.

*   *   *

As soon as Damon heard Lila's scream he forgot everything he ever learned about letting ladies go first. All he knew was that Lila was in danger and the beautiful, wild-eyed woman in front of him was blocking his way.

"Sorry, I have to do this," Damon said. He grabbed her wrists and flung her away from the gate.

"Stop!" the girl screamed as she hit the sidewalk. "Help!"

Damon rushed through the unlocked front gate and began sprinting across the courtyard toward Lila's front door. When he'd returned to town half an hour ago, it took only a moment of Lila's hysterical phone message for him to realize what was going on.

If she'd thought he had been following her and torturing her with crazy phone calls all weekend, it could mean only one thing.

"Lila!" he yelled, skirting one of the courtyard benches and nearly skidding on his side. He pumped his arms and hollered as loud as he could. The thought that his brother was inside Lila's apartment terrified him.

"Let me in!" Damon shouted, working the locked doorknob, then pounding on the door with his fists. "Open this door!"

There was a wrenching, choking scream from inside the apartment. Damon clenched his teeth and rammed his shoulder into the door. Then he took a deep breath and shoved it even harder until the doorjamb began to splinter and break.

"Lila!" he called out, finally flinging open the door and rushing inside the darkened apartment, praying he wasn't too late. He turned the corner into the kitchen, his heart sinking.

"Dylan," he said in a low, warning voice, stepping forward, trying not to let the horrifying scene distract him from what he needed to do.

"Hello there, Damon," Dylan said in the same eerie voice he used to taunt him with when they were growing up. He was sitting on the floor alongside Lila, the knife in his hand pointed directly at her neck. His face, smiling and running with blood, was pressed up next to Lila's so they were sitting cheek to cheek.

Damon sickened at the sight. Lila's feet were bound, and her hands were tied in back of her. Her face, gagged and smeared with blood, was ashen. She looked only half conscious.

"Isn't she beautiful?" Dylan said quietly, turning to stare at Lila. "I'm going to take her away from you, Damon."

"Dylan . . ." Damon took a step forward. Lila's brown eyes were fixed on him now, exhausted and pleading. "What are you doing to Lila? How could you do this?"

Dylan looked thoughtful. He wiped his hand back over his forehead, then stared at the blood on his palm. "You took so many things from me, you know.

257

It's only fair. Mom and Dad gave you everything."

Damon shook his head. "No, Dylan. We just wanted you to be safe. You've been sick. You know that. We've talked to you so many times about it. . . ."

"Shut up!" Dylan suddenly wailed, bringing the knifepoint right against Lila's skin.

Damon stepped forward quickly and kicked the knife out of Dylan's hand. It skittered across the kitchen floor. Dylan rushed for it just as the slender figure of another girl appeared in the doorway.

"Year after year we care for you and help you, and this is what we get in return?" he heard himself shout to his brother as his pent-up anger began to explode. "You're my brother. My own twin. And all you've ever given me is more violence and sickness and horror . . . horror. . . ."

Damon lifted his fist, but Dylan flipped over and rolled out of the way, lunging past the blond girl and into the living room, where the brothers crashed against a cabinet and thundered to the floor—a tangle of thrashing arms and legs.

Chapter Seventeen

"We're getting you out of here, Lila," Jessica cried, dropping to the floor and grabbing the knife. Without hesitation she cut the rope on Lila's feet and hands, then quickly opened the freezer door and hid the knife behind Lila's frozen yogurt.

"Damon . . . ," Lila sobbed incoherently, rubbing her wrists. "I don't understand. . . ."

In the living room Jessica heard the two brothers grappling, smashing furniture and thundering against the walls. She knew she had to get Lila out of the apartment, but when she looked at Lila's face again, she sickened. Lila's face was ashen, as if every ounce of blood had been drained from it. Her blue lips shivered, and she looked as if she were about to pass out.

There was another loud crash, which sounded

like a falling bookcase, followed by more grunting sounds and the ripping of fabric.

Jessica looked up for a moment in intense disgust. It wasn't very long ago that Lila had spent thousands decorating the apartment in imported silk slipcovers, French country antiques, and several museum-quality Chinese porcelains. Now it was being totally *trashed* by these two Neanderthals who had no respect for property!

"Damon," Lila moaned, her head drooping to one side.

Jessica looked back down at her friend. "You need a doctor, Lila," she murmured, springing up to grab the phone. "I'm calling 911. We're going to get the police *and* an ambulance in here right away."

She ducked her head around the corner and looked into the living room, where the two Damons were locked in battle, rolling one over the other toward Lila's patio door, which they smashed.

"This line is dead!" Jessica cried, staring at the silent receiver.

"Jes-si-ca," Lila moaned, falling over on her side in the corner of the kitchen floor. She clutched her chest. "Help."

Jessica looked at her friend on the floor, then she looked through the doorway at the two look-alike Damons, still furiously fighting on Lila's living room carpet. Her whole body began to shake with rage and frustration.

"Get out of here, you maniac!" Jessica shrieked. "I don't care who you are, Damon, Damon, and Damon. . . ."

Jessica gasped as the two Damons began to roll and grapple all over Lila's fabulous eighteenth-century Persian rug, their shirts half torn off, their arms bloodied and bruised. Outraged, she turned and grabbed a heavy Cuisinart sitting on Lila's kitchen counter. For a moment she just stood there, trying to figure out which Damon was just the stupid TA who'd humiliated her in class and which Damon was the knife-wielding maniac who'd attacked Lila at Astra's beach house.

Finally she chose the one with the worst haircut. The guy with the black T-shirt from the beach. Yes, that was the Damon she liked the least. Though she *definitely* didn't like the other one either.

As the two men rolled dangerously close to her she took one step forward, held the Cuisinart out carefully over the correct head, and dropped it.

"Take *that!*" Jessica cried out victoriously as the appliance crashed precisely where she'd aimed it. "Now try not to get blood all over the rug!"

Thump-*thump*. Thump-*thump*. Thump-*thump*.
Though her eyes were closed, Lila was aware of so many things. Her mind was rushing like a swiftly running stream. Memories flashed before her as if they had little time left in her dying brain.

Her childhood pony. Her high-school prom. Her fairy-tale wedding to Tisiano. Bruce.

Damon.

The kitchen floor was so hard and gritty against her cheek. In the background she could hear the deafening sound of the two men fighting and Jessica shouting. Lila groaned and tried to breathe, but the tightness in her chest held her back. Her head felt as if someone had smashed it inside. When she tried to sit up, she immediately wished she hadn't.

"Ohhh," she moaned.

Her head fell back hard, though she suddenly felt as if she were floating. What was happening? Lack of air? Why couldn't she breathe? Her lips were numb. Her fingers wouldn't move.

There was another crash beside her as the two Damons fell back in through the kitchen door. Her eyes fluttered open. Such loud shouting. One Damon had fallen on top of the other's chest, had grabbed hair, and was now slamming the head against the floor, over and over. . . .

Thump-*thump*. Thump-*thump*. Thump-*thump*.

Lila tried to focus. Was she dreaming? Hadn't she been through this before? She remembered the hard kitchen floor, the tightening of her chest, and the sudden flash of the two Theodores above her—struggling.

Was she Flora or Lila now? Was she dreaming her death again? Or was she really Lila, living her last few moments like this, just as Flora had before the hood of darkness dropped and she was sent upward into the beautiful light?

She began to cry softly. Even in the confusion and noise she could feel each tear as it slid down her cheek. Damon's face kept flashing before her. First one Damon, then two. She could have loved him so. They were two halves of a whole. They really, really were. . . .

Lila focused her eyes one last time as her heart began to pound even more fiercely in her ears. Above she could see Jessica moving about, her golden hair swishing, her eyes flashing angrily. Lila watched her pick up something heavy and drop it on the bloodied and black-T-shirted Damon. She wasn't sure what was happening, but there was a moment of blissful silence before the shouting began again.

"Stop, Dylan," she heard her Damon cry out. "Get away from her. You've got to stop."

Lila squinted through her tears, watching as Dylan staggered up from the floor and lunged for Damon a final time. Damon's feet were planted solidly, but his powerful arms still wrestled with his weakened twin, now bleeding profusely from the temple. Lila could see the way Damon looked at his brother, his eyes filled with pain and grief. But the next moment Dylan reached up to scratch at his brother's eyes, and Damon shoved him downward.

Lila watched through the fog of her dreamlike

state. She knew that Jessica was screaming and that Damon was cursing, but nothing seemed to sink in. It was all in slow motion, she thought as she watched Dylan skid backward across the kitchen floor.

She saw the knife glinting there. It was still there, she saw, wedged between the dishwasher and the cabinet, just as Dylan had arranged it for her own neck. He had done a very good job of choosing the very sharpest knife too. She would have picked the same one. The blade tip had been filed to a razorlike point, she remembered. It had hurt so when it had scraped her.

Lila watched Dylan slide. It happened so very slowly. Or was it too quickly? His body seemed to curl slightly so that his back curved and his neck was protruding when it met the tip of the knife.

The blade sank neatly into the back of his neck. Just the way he'd planned it for her own. It went straight through until the tip reappeared again at his throat, and his body went limp.

There was a scream. Her heart galloped in her chest. The fog dropped down again over her eyes, and then there was only velvety darkness.

Flora was floating above a shimmering stretch of green lawn, bordered by giant maples that had turned fiery orange and red in the slanting October sun. Here and there bunches of flowers were laid carefully over the flat stones, each with its own name and date etched in shining granite.

"Here he is," she murmured to herself as the top of Theodore's beloved head came into view. She gazed at it tenderly. Such a beautiful head and face. Such a wonderful, loving husband. Still, she could see that he was not at peace the way she was now.

He was kneeling down, and she drew close, hoping he could sense her presence there. She wanted him to be happy. She wanted to him look around, to smell the grass and the earth and sky while he still could. "Flora," he was whispering.

She moved in closer and smiled when she saw what he was gazing at. Directly in front of her now was a large statue, carved out of the finest, shining white marble. She stared at it with wonder. It was the statue of an angel, her wings outstretched and her long, graceful arms brought together above her head, where she clasped a single rose. She stood on one delicate foot, the other lifted lightly into the air, as if she were reaching for heaven. With indescribable care the sculptor had carved the stone so that she appeared to be wearing a gown as thin as gossamer wings.

Flora floated above him, recognizing the face of the angel as her own. She saw the direct eyes, the uplifted chin, and the hair swirling thickly in stone about her cheeks just as it had when she was alive and together with him.

She looked below at the foot of the statue, where Theodore now laid his head.

FLORA ARMSTRONG GREY
1912–1937
SHE LOVED
SHE INSPIRED
SHE LIGHTS UP THE HEAVENS

Flora stroked his hair when she saw that he was crying bitterly now, and for a moment afterward he seemed to feel her hand. He looked upward, as if he had sensed her presence.

"I'll never forgive my brother for doing this to you, Flora," she heard him whisper. "No matter how far I have to search or how long it takes, I will avenge your death."

"Lila?"

She'd barely opened her eyes, but she was aware of harsh, fluorescent lights above. An antiseptic odor filled her nose. She heard the sound of rolling metal carts and distant, ringing telephones.

"Lila?"

Lila struggled to open her eyes. There was a terrible taste in her mouth, and for a moment she thought she was going to be sick.

"Take your time. You've had a bad shock, and you're in the hospital."

"What . . . ?"

A pleasant woman's face appeared, framed by crisp salt-and-pepper hair. She wore light blue hospital scrubs and had a shiny stethoscope around her neck. "I'm Dr. Wiley," she said quietly. "How are you feeling?"

Lila looked around and took a deep, cleansing breath. "OK," she croaked, though she really wasn't sure.

Dr. Wiley glanced at something up above Lila's head, then made a notation on a clipboard. "You've been heavily sedated for about twelve hours, so you might be feeling a little woozy."

Lila struggled to think. "What—what happened?"

The woman gave her a sympathetic look. "You were brought into the ER last night by ambulance, suffering from some pretty bad cuts and bruises as well as some nasty chest pain and anxiety symptoms."

"My heart," Lila groaned. "I couldn't breathe. My lips were numb. I thought I was dying. . . ."

"Yes," the doctor said calmly, taking her pulse. "It's a common anxiety reaction, although we gave you an EKG and chest X ray to make sure your symptoms were noncardiac in origin."

"Oh, I see," Lila whispered.

"When you hyperventilate like that during times of stress," the doctor explained, "your blood gases go out of whack. Too much oxygen causes the numbness, chest pain, and shortness of breath."

"It was terrible," Lila cried softly.

"You were in bad shape," the doctor said, standing up and smiling. "But the point-five milligrams of Xanax we gave you last night did the trick. It let you get some rest, which is exactly what you needed. It sounds like you've been through an awful lot."

"Yes," Lila said. "Yes, I have."

"Dr. Wiley?"

Lila looked over and saw a nurse in a pink pantsuit standing at the door with a clipboard in hand.

"May Miss Fowler have visitors yet?"

"Yes. She's awake and doing well," Dr. Wiley said as she was leaving. "Come right in."

Lila saw Jessica emerge from behind the nurse, pale and dragged out, as if she hadn't slept all night. Her blond hair was tangled, her eye makeup was smudged, and for the first time Lila could remember, Jessica appeared to be wearing absolutely no lipstick at all. Two of the front buttons on her sweater were unbuttoned, and Lila could see blood spatters and dirt all over her jeans.

"Jessica?" Lila whispered weakly.

"I'm so sorry," Jessica began breathlessly. "It's all my fault. . . ."

"Your fault?" Lila echoed.

"Yes!" Jessica insisted, sliding onto the edge of the bed and rubbing her eyes. "If I hadn't told you about writing that stupid letter to Bruce, you

268

wouldn't have run off like that back to your apartment."

Lila sipped a drink of water the nurse handed her. "I should have stayed with you, Jessica. Especially after Damon's . . . brother attacked me at Astra's."

Jessica's eyes flashed angrily. "I was so freaked by that guy. . . ." She bit her lip and stopped. "But let's talk about that after you're better." She looked over her shoulder, then winked. "There's someone else here to see you, Lila."

"Who?" Lila whispered, just as Damon's face appeared in front of her.

For a split second she felt a rush of doubt and fear. She saw his face in front of her. The same handsome face with its strong jawline and green, searching eyes. She stared at his dark hair and the way it fell so gently over his brow. Then she held out her hand and drew him closer.

"Is it you?" she whispered, brushing the hair off his brow and looking for the tiny scar.

She breathed in, then out again with relief. There was no scar. He was Damon. He was the same Damon she'd fallen in love with.

"Hold me," she said softly, reaching out her arms. "Just hold me."

Chapter
Eighteen

*It's amazing how romantic that kiss is, even with
Lila looking like something the cat dragged in,*
Jessica thought.

Actually, Jessica had to catch her breath as
Damon and Lila shifted their embrace, smiled at
each other, then kissed each other tenderly on the
lips again.

This looks as good as something out of General
Hospital, Jessica decided, though she had to shake
her head with wonder. Lila's arm was taped up
and stuck with an intravenous needle, which
wound its way up to a waggling bag of solution
hovering over the hospital bed. Her wrists were
bandaged, white gauze was wrapped about her
head and neck, and her pale face was nicked and
spotted all over with yellow antiseptic.

Plus, Jessica noted with horror, Lila's gorgeous

hair was completely sweaty and stuck to her head in ropy strands.

Jessica rolled her eyes. *Amazing how love can camouflage even the worst bad hair days,* she mused.

Damon finally stood up and glanced shyly at Jessica. Then he stuck out his hand for her to shake and gave her a tired smile. "I remember you now. You're the one I gave such a bad time before class last week."

"Yes," Jessica quickly. "You did."

"I apologize," Damon said. "I guess I picked up on the tension between you two that day and—"

"I was being a jealous jerk," Jessica interrupted. "Happens all the time. Don't worry about it."

Damon cleared his throat and sat back down at the edge of Lila's bed. "OK, then."

"Jessica's . . . impulsive," Lila said softly. "But I think she came to our rescue last night."

"The Cuisinart," Jessica blurted. "It was just sitting there, and that nasty brother of yours was going to murder all of us. I think I slowed him down a little."

Damon's face turned serious. He squeezed Lila's hand.

Lila paled. "Is he . . . ?"

"He's dead," Damon said softly. He turned away from her and bent over, sinking his face into his hands. Jessica could see that he was crying. "I don't think he suffered. It happened so quickly . . .

with the knife right there the way it was."

Jessica cringed. She was glad she'd left the apartment right after it had happened to call an ambulance for Lila. She was also grateful that Lila had passed out by then, so she didn't have to see the big bloody mess on her kitchen floor.

"I'm so sorry, Damon," Lila was soothing him, stroking his back. "I'm so sorry about your brother. You never told me you had a twin, so I never suspected . . ."

"It's all my fault," Damon sobbed quietly. "I'd seen him only a week or so ago, and his doctor told me that Dylan had been unusually agitated. They wanted to put him on some stronger medication, but I refused to give them permission." Damon grabbed his hair with both fists. "I couldn't stand to see him zonked on drugs like that. He used to be so full of life."

Jessica stared helplessly as Damon sobbed.

"The hospital tried to call me at home to tell me that Dylan broke out," Damon went on. "They would have caught me before I left town, but I hadn't given them my new number in Sweet Valley. And since it was just connected, even directory assistance didn't have it yet."

Lila lifted her head from her pillow. "So you really didn't have a phone when we first met?"

Damon looked confused. "No, Lila. I'd just moved into that place. And the phone company took forever to get me connected."

Lila lay back and stared at the ceiling.

Jessica leaned forward. "What was wrong with your brother, Damon?"

Damon coughed, then raked his hair back with both hands. "He was diagnosed with schizophrenia when we were about sixteen and had to be institutionalized about six months later."

"How awful," Lila murmured.

"Dylan was my identical twin. We didn't have any other brothers or sisters, so we were really close when we were growing up in Connecticut," Damon went on. He smiled sadly. "Dylan was an incredible talent. A wonderful painter and sculptor. When he was twelve, he learned watercolors and began selling his work to art galleries all over New York. I sort of looked up to him. It was Dylan who got me interested in art."

"He said something about your parents sending him home from an academy," Lila said.

"Yeah." Damon sighed. "He always used to go over that when he got agitated. Our parents sent us—in the grand family tradition—to Thomas Anwater Academy when we were fourteen. We both did pretty well in school, especially Dylan. But after a couple of years he started getting in a lot of trouble. He vandalized the school chapel. He attacked a guy in gym. He even stopped showering. And his grades went way down."

"Whew," Jessica whistled.

"He'd get so depressed," Damon explained. "And then the next day he'd be completely happy. The academy finally kicked him out. When he got home, he set the living room drapes on fire and then he tried to kill himself. After that, Mom and Dad sent him to an institution here in California. That's why I wanted to work here. So I could be near him."

"How did he know where you lived?" Lila asked.

"He didn't," Damon explained. "He just came to SVU after he broke out of the institution."

"Then he started spying on us," Lila suggested, "and broke into your apartment as soon as you left town."

Damon nodded sadly. "Dylan was a very smart guy."

"And he placed those phone calls from your place," Lila murmured.

"And stole a car, according to the police." Damon shook his head. "I never should have told him where I worked. I was just so excited and happy to be living near him. I wanted to help."

"I know," Lila soothed.

Damon grimaced. "And now all I have is a dead brother and . . ." He looked at Lila and bit his bottom lip, unable to go on.

After a few moments Damon spoke again. "I flew up to San Francisco over the weekend, Lila. I needed to get away, and I had research I wanted to do at Stanford."

Lila nodded.

"I took the copy of that old article about Flora Grey with me," Damon said. "The one you gave me that night you came to my apartment. The one that said Theodore Grey had been arrested and that Flora's death was being considered a murder."

"We found out she wasn't murdered," Jessica spoke up. "She'd been attacked, but she died of a heart attack."

"Right," Damon said. "I read that too. And it turns out that Theodore Grey had a twin brother also. He was estranged from Theodore, apparently because he was jealous of his brother's success in the art world. Plus Theodore owed him a lot of money."

Jessica gasped. "He had a twin brother just like you?"

Damon nodded. "I guess there was a lot of talk back then that his twin brother had ruined a lot of Theodore's artwork and even attacked Flora. Some people even believe that it was his twin brother who brought on her heart failure."

Lila suddenly sat up in bed, her eyes wide. "It's true. He did have a twin brother. Thomas."

"Yes, Thomas," Damon echoed.

"And he attacked Flora," Lila went on as tears

began to flood her eyes and spill down her cheeks, "just like . . . like I was attacked. Thomas killed her, Damon. He really did. That's why it was so awful when your brother came in and . . ."

"It's OK now," Damon said softly, wrapping his arms around her. "It's OK."

"So horrible," Lila sobbed. "It was so horrible."

Damon rocked Lila back and forth. "Theodore Grey never painted again after Flora died, you know. After September 1937 art historians can't find a single painting."

"How terrible," Jessica said, wiping away a tear. "It must have broken his heart."

"I never knew this, but Theodore died less than a year after Flora did," Damon said. "He gave all his money and paintings away, then drank himself to death, I guess. I don't know what ever happened to his twin brother. Just disappeared, it seems."

Jessica watched as Damon's head dropped onto Lila's lap and he began sobbing bitterly. She stood up, realizing that the two needed to be alone. "I'm going to head back to the dorms, Lila," she whispered. "I'll check on you tomorrow morning."

"Thank you, Jessica," Lila said softly, stroking Damon's head. "Thank you so much."

*   *   *

For a long while Lila felt herself drifting in and out of a peaceful, groggy state somewhere between sleep and consciousness—a deep, dreamless place where there was only rest and security. She could feel Damon's hand in hers and hear the soft rumble of hospital carts in the corridor. When she finally opened her eyes again, she saw that a soft yellow light had filled the room and that Damon had fallen asleep in the chair next to her bed.

As soon as she looked at him he awakened and smiled. "How are you feeling?"

"Fine," Lila answered. "A little afraid to fall asleep."

Damon nodded and looked deep into her eyes. "No bad dreams this time?"

"No bad dreams," Lila whispered.

"I'll never forgive myself for leaving you alone like that."

Lila shifted in the bed, wincing against the pain. Her head throbbed from being thrown against the bedroom wall, and her wrists and ankles ached from being so tightly bound. "Why *did* you have to leave town like that, Damon? It was so sudden."

Damon's face seemed to collapse. "I had to, Lila. I was scared."

"It was so horrible," Lila murmured. "Dylan looked so much like you, and yet I could feel in my heart that he wasn't you. I kept getting his strange, taunting phone calls. He followed me.

He broke into my apartment and did such horrible things. . . ."

Damon threw his arms on the bed, sobbing. "Oh no, Lila. I'm so sorry."

Lila gazed at Damon for a moment. He'd seemed so stern and almost unapproachably academic when she'd first seen him in class. But now she knew he wasn't like that at all. He was a sweet, tender man. A man who'd done everything he could to remain loyal to his brother. "What were you scared of when you left?" she finally asked.

"I was afraid of you," Damon replied. "Or maybe I should say afraid *for* you."

"What?"

Damon leaned forward and crossed his tanned forearms on his knees. "That night you came over to my place after reading about Flora Grey's death in the library . . ."

"What?" Lila prodded.

Damon looked uncomfortable. "You were upset, I realize that. But you were also more than upset. You were so disturbed by your dreams and your feeling of connection with this woman . . ."

"That I pushed all the wrong buttons," Lila finished his sentence, nodding. "I see."

"Didn't you see how angry you made me?" Damon went on. "Don't you remember the way I shook you and called you Flora and frightened you?"

"I remember," Lila reassured him. "I upset you, I guess—"

"But I don't want to ever be upset like that with you—or anyone," he insisted. "Don't you see? Ever since we found out that Dylan was mentally ill, I've had a horrible fear that—that the same thing could happen to me. Or could happen to someone close to me."

Lila nodded. "So when I rushed in and started screaming about nightmares and strange coincidences and how I was worried about getting murdered, you reacted. You thought that maybe I was losing my mind."

"Yes," Damon said seriously. "And not just you. I started acting like a crazy man. You stirred up such feelings in me. I started losing control . . . just like Dylan did."

"But you're not Dylan," Lila said.

"I'll never get away from him, though," Damon insisted, making a fist and staring at it. "I'll always have that fear of losing my mind, like my twin."

"I wish you'd told me," Lila said as a surge of sadness and regret flooded her. "I wish you'd reached out to me."

Damon nodded.

Lila turned on her side. "I talked to a woman yesterday who believes that I might actually be a reincarnation of Flora Grey. I know it sounds

279

crazy, but she doesn't think it's a coincidence that we met and had such an immediate connection. Or that you recognized me from the paintings you loved. Or that I saw the Grey paintings in my dreams first before you ever showed them to me."

Damon's green eyes filled with interest.

"This woman thinks there's a reason I dreamed of events that really happened sixty years ago," Lila said in a trembling voice. "She said it had something to do with the law of karma."

Damon nodded and stared absently into space. "Those who cause suffering in one life must pay in another life. Immoral or violent acts are always avenged, even if it takes forever."

"Yes," Lila exclaimed. "That's what she said."

"I'm not sure, Lila." Damon stared down at his hands. "Nothing makes sense to me anymore."

"Theodore vowed that he would avenge Flora's death by harming his brother, no matter how long it took," Lila whispered. "I think that's what happened when your brother died last night. The same events played out, only the outcome was different."

Damon squeezed Lila's hand. "I'll think about it. But all that's important to me now is I never let anything like this happen to you again."

Lila closed her eyes, and for one wonderful second she imagined what it would be like to fall in love with Damon all over, starting from scratch. But she realized right then that they could never start over. The past would always be there, haunting them and keeping them apart.

Choking back tears, Lila felt her heart ripping in two as she looked into his handsome, earnest face. "It won't happen again."

He shook his head. "Never again."

Lila took a deep breath. "Because I can't see you again, Damon."

She watched as Damon's eyes widened in shock. He took her hand and grasped it. "What are you talking about? I love you, Lila. I want to be with you."

"No," she said firmly, though her heart was breaking. "It will never work. Not after what we've been through. I know it in my heart."

Damon rubbed his eyes. "Lila . . ."

Lila felt her eyelids getting heavier. "I know it's right, Damon. We'd always have this horrible memory connecting us and pulling us down. It would never work, no matter how hard we tried."

Damon kissed her lips. "I'll try to live with that, Lila. But . . . isn't there anything I can do for you? I can't leave you right now."

Lila caught his mouth and kissed him again. "Just stay with me for a little while. I'm so tired, but I'm still so afraid to sleep. The nightmares . . ."

Damon reached over and stroked her hair. "I'll stay here for as long as you need me. Close your eyes."

*   *   *

When Lila opened her eyes again, the hospital room was very dark. She might have felt that she was completely alone and scared in the world if she hadn't seen Damon's face in a pool of light next to her bed. He was sitting in a flimsy chair, his head thrown back and his eyes closed in a deep sleep.

Slowly she moved her hand toward him until she brushed the side of his arm and he stirred.

"Hi," she said.

He nodded awake. "Hi." He looked at his watch. "It's eight P.M. You slept for most of the day."

Lila looked over at the dark window. The striped curtain around the bed. The big TV poised at the top of the wall. Solid things. Real things. She sighed. "I slept really well. For the first time in ages."

Damon sat up straight and rubbed his chin. "No nightmares?"

Lila grinned. "Nope."

"What are you smiling at?"

Lila stretched out her hands, careful not to pull the IV still in her arm. "Something feels different, that's all. Maybe it's over. Maybe Flora can rest in peace now."

"And you can too," Damon said. He stood up and kissed her forehead tenderly, then stepped back and stuck his hands in his pockets. "Are you OK?"

Lila nodded, pressing her lips together.

"Should I go now?" His look seemed to take in every inch of her face.

"Yes. It's time," Lila said quietly. "I know it sounds crazy, but I feel as if Flora's death has been avenged. That was our purpose together. I really do believe that's why we met."

"Maybe you're right," Damon said, gently taking her hand and kissing it before turning to leave.

Lila watched the door to her hospital room open. Then Damon's tall figure slipped through the wedge of light and into the hallway, out of her life forever. A tear slid down her cheek, and for a few moments she simply lay there, savoring the solid feeling of peace in her heart that had been missing for so long.

Then with a swift, sure movement she reached for her purse, which Jessica had brought for her from home. Inside, she quickly found the thick black address book in which she had so carefully written Bruce's phone number in Japan.

It's time to deal with your life again, Lila, she told herself as a warm glow began to spread through her body. *After all, it's the only life you have.*

Or was it?